THE
SECRETS
OF THE
DREAM MASTER

BY: C.M. Prince

ISBN: 979-8-9993912-2-3

Library of Congress Control Number: 2025916646

Author photo taken by: Melanie Becker

Cover design by: Shema (create_shema via Fiverr)

Editors: Vicky Skinner & Roxana Coumans

To Danielle Bedingfield, whose character was at the heart of this story's earlier version.

Acknowledgments

This book would not have been possible without the support, encouragement, and inspiration from so many incredible people in my life.

First and foremost, I'm thankful to God for having this opportunity to publish this book and being able to continue writing. I'm especially thankful to my amazing wife, Krissy Prince, for her unwavering love and belief in me. You've been my rock and my biggest supporter every step of the way.

To my family: my mom, Carol Prince, and my sister, Sarah Christiansen, along with her family: thank you for always standing by me and cheering me on in every endeavor.

To my "sister from another mister," Melanie Becker, and her family, your constant support and encouragement have meant the world to me.

A special thank you to Chloe Schlabach, Kelsie Lamb, Makayla Edwards, and Renata Pfister. When I found myself stuck, your insights and creative ideas helped me move forward and brought this book to life. A couple of those ideas were the missing puzzle pieces I needed, and I'm so grateful for your help in making this story a reality!

To everyone who has walked this journey with me, thank you for believing in me and in this story. This book exists because of you.

Table of Contents

Chapter 1

The First Dream

The First Dream

"Where am I?" I say aloud, my voice echoing in every direction. The place is unfamiliar, nothing but endless white stretches out as far as I can see. Wherever this is, I feel cold and lost. I slowly start to walk, having no sense of direction. Even though I walk for a few minutes, it feels as if I have barely taken a few steps. After realizing that it seems pointless to walk, I start to yell in the hopes that I'm not alone in this unorthodox place.

"Hello! Is there anyone out there?" I repeat this at least a dozen times, hoping I'm not alone.

Out of breath from yelling at the top of my lungs, the panic starts to set in. I run as fast as I can. I still have no idea where I'm going, just pushing forward through this endless void. Then I stop. My lungs are on fire, sweat clings to my skin. It's at that moment I realize something strange. In this place, there is no sound except for the ones I make. My voice, my footsteps, my breathing; those are the only things breaking the silence. If I stay perfectly still or stop breathing, it feels like I've gone completely deaf. What is happening?

Unsure of what to do next, I sit down on the ground. Time seems to blur around me. I have no idea how long I've been sitting here, but if I had to guess, it feels like hours. I just stare straight ahead, my mind strangely blank. I don't know why I can't think or focus. I'd usually be thinking of an escape plan or, at the very least, wondering where I am. Neither of those things are happening. I can't conjure any type of plan, period. What am I supposed to do? I don't even know where I am. Am I outside? Am I inside somewhere? Am I in a room? There's only one thing I know for certain about this place: I want to leave.

The urge to leave hits me so hard that I start to have a massive panic attack. I'm having trouble catching my breath. I gather myself and get up and take off running. I run for what seems like an hour. I'm out of breath, freaking out more than ever now. I have to stop. I cannot continue to run. Then, while I stand there bent over, trying to catch my breath, I notice someone off in the distance.

"What?" I say to myself.

I don't know what to think. Should I feel relieved that someone else is here, or afraid because I have no idea what they want? They are too far away for me to make out any details, but I can tell this person is walking toward me.

I look down for just a moment to steady myself. When I look back up, the person is much closer, maybe only half the distance from before. My heart jumps. There's no way they could have covered that much ground so quickly. They are still far enough that I could run if I needed to, but close enough to make me uneasy. Something feels off.

I try to run, but my body is frozen. No matter how hard I try to get away, it is to no avail. It's not fear holding me back. I'm straining every muscle in my body, desperately trying to move. It feels like sleep paralysis, except I'm fully awake and standing still. Despite this, the person keeps coming closer to me. My fear intensifies. I don't know what this person wants or why they're walking toward me. Given the situation, I assume the worst. This person wants to hurt me. I push myself even harder to move, but I'm wearing myself out.

I slowly stop making any attempts to move. I realize then that I have no choice but to let whatever is going to happen, happen. The person approaches even closer, but my fear is diminishing. The person is a young boy. My fear now turns into confusion. I have no idea what to expect. Why is he here? Why am I here? How is he able to move while I'm frozen? He continues to move toward me slowly. This little boy, with pale skin and brown hair and a yellow onesie, is just walking; he does not even talk while he is moving. He does not wave or give me any kind of signal. As he comes closer, I start to notice his facial expressions, and they begin to make me feel uneasy again. He looks scared, tired. He looks as if he has not slept in years. Maybe that's why he is walking so slow.

Perhaps he is frightened of me. However, he keeps walking toward me. It wouldn't make sense for him to fear me. That's when it strikes me. If he's not scared of me, then he's afraid of someone or something else. I'm now terrified at the thought that someone or something is in this space with us. No, there cannot be someone else here. I would hear them… Wait, that is right. The sounds coming from my mouth and body are the only sounds I can hear. So, I wouldn't hear things like footsteps against the floor, or whatever this is we are walking on. The longer I stay in this place, the more terrified I become.

The young boy comes within six feet of me, then stops. He stands there, staring at me. I'm still frozen. I try with all my might to move. I feel as if I have suddenly become a statue and that there is no way for me to get out of that position. All I can do is stare straight into this young boy's green eyes. It feels a bit intimidating, staring into someone's eyes for that long. As I panic and try to figure out what to do next, I notice the young boy slowly opening his mouth to speak.

"Hel…" he whispers very softly.

I finally am able to move. It feels so good to move again. I start to step in closer because I can't fully make out what the young boy is telling me.

"What are you trying to say?" I ask him.

"Hel…" he whispers again, making it very difficult to understand what he is trying to tell me.

Is he saying Hell? I'm not sure, but it certainly feels like we are in some type of Hell in my book.

I try again. "Hell? Are you trying to say Hell?"

The boy, whose facial expressions are as puzzling as this whole environment we are in, starts to speak again.

"Help."

Help. That's what he's trying to say. Now, I'm in a precarious situation. I want to ask him why he needs help. I'm afraid of what his answer will be. However, being the only adult in this place, I feel I have no other choice but to ask.

"Why do you need help? Do you need help getting out of here? Is someone hurting you?" I ask, faking as much confidence as possible.

He looks at me, his eyes beginning to well up. This time, his voice grows a little louder as he speaks. "He's coming after me."

One of my fears about this place has been realized. There is someone else here. Again, I display my fake confidence and start to ask him more questions.

"Where is he? Why is he coming after you?" I ask, partly because I want answers, but also with a sense of regret, wondering if maybe I'm better off not knowing. Especially in a place as strange as this.

As the mysterious young boy starts to speak, the ground begins to shake violently. The trembling is intense, far worse than any earthquake I've ever experienced. The ground rumbles beneath us with such force that we lose our balance and are thrown to the ground. Strangely, the shaking stops just as suddenly as it began. Then, without warning, a deep and terrifying voice echoes through the air, as if coming from nowhere and everywhere at once. It speaks three chilling words:

"DO NOT INTERFERE!"

The boy immediately breaks down, crying out in loud, frightened wails. I reach out, trying to comfort him, but the violent shaking returns. It's stronger than before. Lying on the ground, I can feel every tremor hammering through my body. Just as suddenly as it returned, the shaking stops again. A massive shadow begins to stretch over us, growing larger with every second. Before I can even see what is casting it, I wake up.

Chapter 2

Just the Beginning

My eyes slowly open as I lie here in my bed, awakening from the horrific nightmare. It's 3 AM and now I feel like I can't go back to sleep. I look over to my right hand, which has torn a hole in the sheet during the dream. I've never had a dream that caused me to do something like this. Never has my whole body reacted to a dream like this. I lie in bed, staring at the ceiling fan, which spins slowly overhead as the streetlight pokes through the curtain, shining brightly in my face. I can hear the cars rushing by my apartment and the sirens from fire trucks as they speed to a fire. My body feels like it is encased in stone, each movement a struggle against unrelenting stiffness. My bloodshot eyes, raw and tired, sting as I try to blink away the memories of the night. The dream lingers like a shadow, each fragmented image clawing at my nerves, leaving me jittery and haunted.

I decide to go ahead and get out of bed. I grab my laptop from the floor and start to look over my resume. I'm in the process of looking for another job. The thought of finding a new job weighs on my mind, even as my current role at the University of

Oxford continues to anchor me here in Oxford. Though my work has taken me far and wide, I still hope to return to Georgia, where I was born and raised.

I read to myself the beginning part of my resume to ensure that I have my personal information correct. "Name, Geneva Koraline. Date of birth, June 21, 1986. Current home, Kennington, England, UK. Profession: Psychologist. Education, BS in Psychology, Master's in Psychology, and Psy.D." I stop looking at my resume. I decide that I have plenty of time to look this over. I need to finish grading papers from my classes. However, I always end up getting distracted when grading papers, so we'll see how long this actually lasts. I love to teach, but I'm also hoping to get back to meeting with clients and working with people who are in desperate need of help. I'm looking forward to getting back into the field. I know I'll have to get licensed again, but I'm willing to put in the work.

I decide to binge a series I've been meaning to finish for a while. Guess I found my distraction. I do this until it's time to start getting ready for work. Despite everything I do this morning, I still cannot get that dream out of my head. At one point while I'm binge-watching, I decide to write down the dream and all the details. I want to remember this bizarre nightmare. I arrive at work at 7 AM. I don't have any classes to teach today, but I'll be helping some students who need assistance with their research projects. As soon as I sit down at my desk in my office, the phone starts ringing. Well, looks like today is going to be a busy day.

"This is Dr. Koraline from the Psychological Department. How may I help you?"

After getting off the phone, I notice some of my students passing by my office. I'm currently the department head of psychological studies, and everyone knows me from my research on dreams and subconscious activity. I've always been interested in dreams and why we have them. I know there are answers as to why we dream, but I've always wondered if there is more we do not yet understand.

I'm proud of my contributions to the scientific understanding of dreams. My work delves into how dreams reflect our subconscious, process emotions, and contribute to creativity and problem-solving. By exploring the intricate connection between our waking lives and the dream world, I aim to uncover the deeper meanings behind these nightly narratives and how they influence our personal growth and mental health. It's inspiring to know that my research helps people better understand the mysteries of their inner worlds and how dreaming shapes our experiences.

"Dr. Koraline, may I reference your lectures at the Science Convention in St. Louis last year for help with my research paper?" asks a student who passes by my office.

"Yes, you can. You can reference as many as you like. Just remember your reference page this time!" I respond.

I enjoy working with my students and I love my job. I want people to recognize the power of the subconscious mind. I wish I could tap into people's subconscious, just enough for me to see what's going on in their minds. My work draws attention from around the world, particularly from various governments. While their intentions are often unclear, I get approached multiple times for consultation on classified projects. I've only agreed to three. These are chosen because they provide full transparency about their goals and expectations. I'm against most governmental uses of my research and firmly believe it should remain in the public domain rather than hidden behind classified restrictions.

A few hours later, I lock my office up and take a nap. I dream about the ability to see into people's minds and then telling patients that everything will be okay, telling them that I feel the pain they see in their dreams. Though I often dream about my work, I'm still shaken by the dream I had this morning.

My nap is interrupted by the sound of the office phone ringing off the hook. I look at the Caller ID. I expect it to be one of the professors under me in the department, calling to update me on an ongoing project. However, I see it's an international phone call.

I pick up the phone. "This is Dr. Koraline from the Psychological Department; how may I help you?"

"The following is an international call from Washington, DC, USA."

Oh no. This only means one thing.

My heart sinks and butterflies start flying around in my stomach. I try everything humanly possible to think positive, hoping that this is perhaps another professor calling about my work. Perhaps this is the US Government asking for consultation on a project the public knows about.

I press one to accept the call.

"Hello Dr. Koraline, I'm very thankful you accepted my call," says the voice on the other end.

"Who are you?" I ask very nervously, not knowing what to expect.

"I'm Secretary Travis Jones, head of the US Department of Homeland Security."

"Why are you contacting me?" I ask.

"Dr. Koraline, we need your help with a project that has been personally authorized by the president. Given that you are one of very few people with the necessary expertise, you have been ordered to report in Washington for a briefing with me. After that, you will be taken to the project site."

My stomach sinks. Throughout my entire career, I've never been ordered to take on a project by a head of state.

"I'm very picky about which inquiries I accept. I must inform you that I've only accepted three out of ninety-eight requests. Can you give me justified reasons as to why this should be my fourth?" I say this on the phone, but unlike the dream, I'm very stern and not faking my confidence.

"This is coming straight from the president. Also, to sweeten the pot, you would be given five years of funding to help you restart your 'Dreams Initiative' that you started years ago but had to stop due to funding."

I sit down. I can't believe what I'm hearing. Will they really give me funding for my initiative?

The Dream Initiative is a groundbreaking global project I've been trying to launch. It's dedicated to unlocking the mysteries of the human mind by making it possible to visualize, record, and share dreams. Using cutting-edge neurotechnology (and technology that I'm working with others to try and create), this initiative transforms dream data into vivid, coherent projections that people can experience and explore while awake. To put it simply, this initiative helps people see each other's actual dreams.

"Ok Mr. Secretary, you have my attention. What is this about?"

"This is a matter of national security."

What in the world? What "matter of national security" needs me, especially my expertise? However, the offer of my initiative making a comeback has gotten its grip on me.

"Okay, I'll do this, but you must give me something. What is this project? Why is it a matter of national security? Or is that a ruse to make me feel compelled to work on this project?"

"I wish I could, but due to the nature of the project and for security reasons, I can only give you this information in person. I will explain more when you arrive in Washington. You will be escorted by American Embassy officials to our embassy in London, then to Heathrow to return to America."

He hangs up the phone.

I sit there in disbelief, wondering what in the world is so important that they got the president involved. I look at my phone. I can't believe that it's already 11:30 AM.

Not long after getting off the phone, a woman in business attire knocks on my door. I open the door and she begins to speak.

"Dr. Koraline, you've been asked by the Director of MI6, Nicole Lynne, to meet her outside."

What now? What's going on? I stand there, staring blankly at the wall. I can't process all of this at once.

"Go outside at once. Director Lynne is waiting," she emphasizes. "She's standing next to a black BMW."

I leave abruptly, rushing toward the entrance, and I see a black BMW waiting for me. Director Lynne is standing outside the car. I don't find it a coincidence that she shows up right after I receive that phone call from Washington.

I get into the car. "Before you say anything, I must ask these questions. Why are you here? Does this have to do with…?" Before I can finish, she starts talking.

"I'm talking to you before you are taken to the American Embassy in London," she says.

Ok, this tells me that she knows what's going on. She and her agency must have been listening in on that phone call.

"Okay, why are you getting in contact with me?"

"Dr. Koraline, I'm personally getting in touch with you because we have a bad feeling about the project your government wants you back for."

"How do you even know about this project?"

"We've been monitoring chatter from American Intelligence," Director Lynne begins, her expression tense. "We have not uncovered much about the project so far, but a few months ago, we discovered that several psychologists and psychiatrists from our country and the Commonwealth, all with connections to the US government, were quietly instructed to either take part or provide assistance to this classified initiative. One of them provided us with intel that was nearly incomprehensible; it defied logic and challenged everything we knew. Given its scale and implications, we started tracking those likely to be contacted next, and your work made you a strong candidate. We monitored potential communications and recently confirmed you'd be approached today. I was on my way to brief you, but once I arrived, I was informed that Washington had already contacted you."

I have so many questions. I'm not sure which ones I should try to ask next. So, I go with the logical one.

"What is this project? What are they working on that it 'defies logic' and 'challenged' everything you knew?"

Director Lynne sits back, sighs, and starts talking again. "This will sound ridiculous. However, some of our intel is coming from trusted sources. The US government…" She sighs again. "…is trying to create a machine that can bring dreams to life."

What in the world? This cannot be right. There's no way. How would they even do this? Could their intel be wrong? It must be. There's simply no way that this can be done. If this is indeed true, why is the government interested in this? What possible benefit could it have for them? Well, I can think of plenty, but even so, it feels impossible.

I don't realize that, while I'm thinking about all of this, I'm sitting here in the car, quiet, my mouth dropped open.

"Are you okay?" asks the Director.

"I don't know. I honestly don't know. I'm just trying to process the fact that you just told me that the US government is trying to bring dreams to life."

After answering her question, I start to think about my response. Did I just say that out loud? Bringing dreams to life? So unreal. Though, the thought does cross my mind; are they actually attempting this, or is it a cover for something else?

"I know it's plenty to take in. Trust me, I'm still not fully understanding this whole ordeal. We're working day and night to find out as much as we can," says Director Lynne, who I suspect is about to ask me to do something to help them out. So instead of waiting around to see if I'm right, I decide to ask first.

13

"What do you need me to do? I'm sure that you are not just here to warn me," I tell the director.

"You're very perceptive, Dr. Koraline. Yes, if possible, could you send us any information about the project?" Director Lynne says it in a way that makes me think she's expecting I'll accept this without question. Is she just as crazy as Secretary Jones?

"No disrespect, but they've promised to back my lifelong dream for five years if I go back to help on this project. I risk losing this opportunity. What's in it for me if I get caught?" I say with a bit of frustration in my voice.

Director Lynne looks taken aback. I suspect she wasn't expecting me to have my own demands.

"We will match the offer the US government promised you," Director Lynne says. "My superiors won't be pleased, but I'll do what I must. I know it's a lot to ask, but we're deeply concerned about this project. Other nations, like France and Italy, are quietly expressing similar concerns. All we know for certain is its name: Lion's Tears."

I sit back in the seat, thinking about what she just said. I don't even know how to process what I've been told about this project, but now she wants me to report back to MI6? That would make me a spy, and that's something I didn't sign up to be. But what if this is a cover for something else? Also, the project name, Lion's Tears… What kind of name is that?

We both sit quietly, so I take that time to figure out what I want to do.

"Director, this is what I'll do. I will not give information unless I feel that this project has sinister implications or uses.

However, I also feel that if that's the case, someone in the US should know, too."

"Dr. Koraline, informing anyone in the US is your prerogative. However, you can't disclose to anyone that you're talking with us. Here's what I'll do. I'll give you this secure laptop. Use it for communication with me and, if needed, our agents in the States." Director Lynne then proceeds to pull out the laptop.

"Alright, I'll take the laptop. Please do understand, me taking this laptop is not an agreement to pass along information. I'll keep it if reason compels me to get in contact with you," I tell her, my tone a little sharp. I don't like feeling used.

"Fair enough. We don't want to put any unnecessary tasks on you during this stressful time. However, if you have anything you want to tell us, please be in touch." Director Lynne looks down at her phone.

"I have been informed that the embassy staffers are five kilometers out. Okay, I have to get going. Good luck, and inform us, please."

She hurries me out of the car and then speeds away.

What just happened? What have I gotten myself into? I stand there, wondering about all of this. I decide to go back inside so as not to arouse suspicion. When I come back in, I seek out one of my closest coworkers, Steven.

Steven is in the break room getting coffee, so he's an easy find for me.

"Hey, Steven, come to my office."

"Is everything okay, Dr. Koraline?"

"Just come to my office."

Steven follows me into my office and I close the door.

"Listen, Steven, I have no idea how long I'll be gone."

"Gone? Where are you going? What's going on?" His face shows concern as he asks.

"I've been called back to the United States for something work-related. I don't have all the details yet, but I've been told it's important, and I need to leave as soon as possible. I need you to make sure everything gets done until I return. I have no idea how long that'll be. Keep everything going until I return."

Steven hesitates for a moment before leaving the office. "Well... I hope everything goes smoothly for you," he says, offering a faint smile that does little to hide the concern in his eyes. He doesn't press for details, but I can tell he is worried about the suddenness of my departure.

About five minutes later, two people enter my office: a man and a woman.

"Dr. Koraline, we're with the American Embassy in London. We're escorting you to London. First, we will go to your apartment so you can pack your things," says the man. He's a tall man with dark brown skin, brown eyes, and short black hair. His strong build and posture hint at a military background. The other staffer, a white woman with a fair complexion, stands just a bit shorter. She has shoulder-length black hair and vivid green eyes.

I soon follow them to the car and get into the backseat. As the car drives away from the university, I look back at the place I've worked at for the past three years. I wonder if I'll ever be back here again.

Chapter 3

Shrouded in Mystery

We pull up to my apartment and I walk inside. I have lived here for three years, and I still catch myself calling it an apartment. The word "flat" just doesn't feel natural. I can still picture the amused looks and the usual "You must be from America" remarks. The memory makes me smile, just enough humor to momentarily pull my thoughts away from everything that has happened in the last hour and a half. It's around 2 PM now.

As I enter my apartment, I find the biggest suitcase I have and get to work. I decide to take a week's worth of clothes. I figure that I can attempt to do laundry while I'm there. At least, I hope I can. However, it isn't just the laundry factor that causes me to pack only a week's worth. I also decide that if I only bring a week's worth of clothes, it'll help my mind stay positive in the belief that maybe I won't be gone for too long. My wardrobe primarily consists of a mix of versatile clothing that blends both casual and semi-formal styles. Most of my collection includes classic jeans for everyday wear, dress pants that can easily transition from a relaxed outing to a more polished setting, and shirts that strike the perfect balance between laid-back comfort and sophistication.

After packing my clothes, I go to my office space and grab a few flash drives that contain research I've done over the past five years. I have everything on the cloud, but considering the private nature of this project, I figure I might not be able to easily access my cloud accounts to retrieve it. Though, if I'm being completely honest, I don't even know what research I'm supposed to bring! I don't even believe that this project is possible to achieve. I don't know how I can be of any help at all. I stop for a second. I want to slow down and think. Though I'm certain this project will not be possible, what would I bring to this project?

Once I begin thinking about it this way, I gradually consider what aspects of my research might be relevant. That's when I realize my research into brain activity during dreams could be helpful. How helpful? We'll find out. I place my flash drives in a plastic bag and place them in my suitcase. I stand at the front door of my apartment and look back. I'm not sure how long I'll be gone. What will happen in the next 24 to 48 hours? I have no clue. I leave my apartment and head back to the parked car. I get back inside. The two people who are escorting me are still in the car. We barely spoke on the way here. I decide to strike up a conversation with them.

"What are both of your names?" I ask.

The driver responds first. "I'm Chris."

The person in the passenger seat then responds, "I'm Lea."

"Ah, well, good to meet the two of you, Chris and Lea," I say to them.

They don't respond. I'm not sure what they are thinking about or if they're even paying any attention to me. We're not too far from London itself. So, I'm thinking that if it stays quiet the rest of the way, at least it won't be awkward for too long. However, the conversation does start up about twenty minutes after we leave my apartment. The conversation, however, does not involve me; it's between Chris and Lea. I'm not paying much attention at first because I'm almost falling asleep on this car ride. However, they start talking about something that sparks my interest instantly.

"So, Lea, what's the weirdest dream you've ever had? Because no matter how strange yours might be, I promise the one I had last night was on a whole different level!" Chris says, wide-eyed and looking genuinely freaked out.

This is of great interest to me.

"Chris, I doubt it! The dream I had last night was the weirdest one I've ever had!" Lea responds.

Chris looks at her with a puzzled look. "Stop playing. You're telling me we both had weird dreams last night?"

"I suppose so," responds Lea. "However, I doubt yours was as weird as mine!"

Okay already! Someone needs to start talking. What are their dreams about?

"I doubt it. I'll tell you about mine," Chris continues. "The environment of this dream is weird. I can't comprehend what's going on. I'm underwater, but here's the weird part: I can breathe just fine, even though it still feels like I'm actually underwater."

"Umm, what?" responds Lea, puzzled.

"You know the feeling of being underwater? Now imagine that, but instead of having to hold your breath, you can breathe like normal. So, I would equate it to being in Florida, Louisiana, or South Texas in the middle of summer with all the humidity. You know how hard it is to breathe in those humid environments," says Chris.

"I see," Lea replies, as it appears she is beginning to fully envision the setting of Chris's dream.

I start to think back to the times I've visited Florida in the summer. As much as I love Florida, it's miserable when you aren't on the beach or in the water. I continue listening to Chris's dream.

"Anyway, I start to walk around. The surface I'm walking on reminds me of a pool. However, unlike a pool, I don't see any walls. It just goes on forever, it seems like. I look up. I can't even see any source of light, but light is coming from somewhere. It's a mysterious setting that I can't comprehend. I start to walk, but it's difficult. I even attempt to run, but that's even harder to do. I keep struggling to breathe, constantly feeling like the ability to miraculously breathe underwater could vanish at any moment. I decide that since I'm having difficulties trying to walk or run, I'll attempt to swim toward the surface. Though I can breathe, it's still so difficult!"

I'm intrigued. I can easily imagine the environment, but it's still very weird. This is the first time I've heard a description of a dream so vivid that I can imagine it myself. He continues describing his dream.

"I feel like I swim up at least twenty feet, but I start to get tired. I'm so tired that I start to sink back down, but here's the crazy part. When I sink back down, I'm at the bottom where I started, pretty much instantly! It's like I didn't go anywhere."

"This sounds crazy. It's like there is no escape!" says Lea.

Chris continues, "When I reach the bottom, I'm not just trying to catch my breath, it feels impossible to do so. It's like trying to breathe in the thickest humidity you could ever imagine. Despite all of this, it still isn't the weirdest or craziest part of the dream."

My interest is piqued even more. So far this dream already has plenty of strange elements; I can't imagine what else could top what I've heard.

"In the distance, I see what looks like a small boy," Chris says.

Did he just say a small boy? No, there's no way. It isn't possible. It can't be the same boy I dreamed about, could it? No! It's impossible! I decide to speak up.

"I'm curious, what did the boy look like?" I ask, not knowing what the response will be.

Chris stops and starts to think. It only takes him a few seconds to come up with the answer, but it feels like an eternity. "He has pale skin and brown hair. The thing that stands out to me is what he's wearing."

After Chris says that, my stomach just sinks. I'm having this fear that somehow our dreams are connected. Chris continues to talk about the boy: "He was wearing a pink onesie."

A pink onesie? He was wearing a yellow one in my dream. Maybe, just maybe, this is a very coincidental situation and I'm worrying too much. I suppose I'll just listen to the rest of what he has to say and see.

Chris starts to talk about what the boy was doing. "He won't come to me. I have to walk over to him. I'm still out of breath from trying to escape earlier. I make my way over to him, thinking that he can explain where we are. It takes me a good few minutes to get to him. He doesn't budge at all. He's still, silent, and it takes me a while to get him to look at me. I ask him where we are and how do we get out of here. He just looks at me, and he starts to say something. I think at first, he's trying to say…'"

"Hell. You thought he was trying to say Hell, didn't you?" I cut him off, unable to hold back any longer. I'm already too far into this to stay silent. I expect Chris to say no. But what he says next pulls me even deeper into the mystery.

"Yes! That's what I thought he was saying, but he's actually saying, 'Help me.' I try to get him to tell me why he needs help. I want to say that I ask because I want to help. I honestly ask because I want to know if I'm in danger in whatever this place is! Dr. Koraline, how did you know that?"

I can't wrap my head around the fact that this same boy appeared in both of our dreams.

"That boy was in a dream of mine last night," I say.

Lea looks at Chris. She suddenly has this look of absolute terror on her face. I'm not quite sure why Lea looks so concerned.

She starts to talk. "I'm about to make this even more creepy than it already is." Her voice is trembling a little bit. "I also have a dream with a boy with pale skin and brown hair. However, in my dream, he's wearing a black onesie, and I'm all by myself in the middle of the desert. However, the place I'm in looks familiar. It looks like White Sands National Monument in southern New Mexico. I went there for my sixteenth birthday as part of a trip around the country. The difference is, it seems like the sand dunes go on forever. There he is, just standing there on top of one of the dunes."

Chris and I are attempting to process this information. Chris looks at both of us one at a time.

Chris interrupts, "By any chance, did some shadowy figure attempt to get near to both of you, and tell you…"

"Do not interfere?" Lea and I say at the same time.

The car is completely silent. Neither of them knows anything about this project, but the fear in their eyes makes it clear just how terrified they are by what they've just heard and discovered. The silence lasts for about five minutes. Chris breaks the silence.

"I wonder who he's afraid of. She sounds like a horrible person."

"She?" I ask.

"Yes, her. Why are you asking that?" Chris responds.

"In my dream, he says he's afraid of 'him.' Could you be wrong?" I say.

"I'm certain the voice of the shadow is deep, but it also has a strong woman's voice. The mixture sounds so unique but terrifying," Chris recalls.

"The boy says 'him' in my dream," I respond. "Lea, what does he say in your dream?"

Lea stares at the ground for a few seconds. She responds with an answer that deepens this mystery even more. "He tells me he's scared of them both."

Silence once again comes over the car. You can see that all three of us are trying to interpret what we've all just heard. What in the world is going on? I need answers ASAP! Questions start to rush through my mind as I try to process everything that I've heard. I don't even know what to think or how to feel. Then, a terrifying thought starts to come to my mind. What if this machine is somehow manipulating our dreams? So many unanswered

23

questions. I must get to the bottom of this when I arrive back in the states!

As we begin to enter the London area, I know it won't be long before we reach the embassy. I can't help but wonder whether anyone else there knows about the project, or if it's being kept between just a select few.

Chapter 4

The Nightmare Flight

We eventually arrive at the embassy; I'm taken aback at how this building looks. I've seen some interesting building designs throughout my life, but this by far has to be one of the most interesting. I know I've never been to this part of London because I would remember seeing this odd building. The embassy is designed as a cube-shaped structure surrounded by a dazzling glass exterior, showcasing a distinctive crystalline pattern with angled panels. Surrounding the structure is a gorgeous park that has reflective pools, pathways, and gardens. It's a beautiful but intriguing building.

"Yeah, that's everyone's reaction when they first see this unique building," says Chris, who's reading my facial expressions via the rearview mirror. "This building is relatively new," continues Chris. "I have mixed reactions about the design."

"Don't we all?" asks Lea. I can tell she is not a fan of the design choices either.

We park and go inside; the interior looks even more interesting. I can't get over this place. Lea instructs me to sit on this modern-looking black couch in the lobby. She and Chris then disappear around a corner. On the wall to my right is a giant version of the US Seal. They definitely want you to know what embassy you're in. There is a good amount of activity around the embassy, as I watch about sixty people walk past me in five minutes. I try to play on my phone to distract myself from what is happening around me. However, it only works so much as I continue to dwell on what has taken place so far. It still feels unreal that I arrived at work this morning and now I'm about to be on a plane to DC.

Ten minutes later, a man rounds the corner with Lea and Chris. From across the lobby, this man strikes me as an imposing figure; not just for his height but his composed, confident demeanor. His perfectly tailored suit hints at professionalism, while his pale complexion contrasts with its dark tones. He wears glasses that do not quite fit, constantly adjusting them as he walks toward me.

"Dr. Koraline, I'm Nicolas Bowen. I'm here to give you some instructions on what to do next. I'm giving you a boarding pass to fly from Heathrow to Washington Dulles. There, you'll be picked up from the airport and taken straight to Secretary Jones."

"So, what now? Are Chris and Lea taking me to the airport?" I ask.

"Yes," replies Nicolas. "They'll drop you off there, and you'll check in your stuff. I believe they paid for up to three bags. If you have more, you'll have to pay out of pocket."

I pack everything into a carry-on and in suitcase, preparing for just a week. This makes me question whether I should have packed for a longer trip.

"Okay, what time is my flight?" I ask.

"You leave in two and a half hours, so 9:30. We better get you going.

Nicolas hands me the boarding pass and Chris and Lea lead the way. They're moving at a bit of a hurried pace so I keep up. Once we get in the car and start making our way to Heathrow, it's even more silent than when we were inside. It's as if Chris and Lea are processing everything as well. The car ride to London opens my eyes to numerous things.

The first thing it opens my eyes to is the fact that British Intelligence may be right. I really thought that they were insane for suggesting that the US is trying to make a machine that can turn dreams into reality. However, seeing how interconnected our dreams are, it makes me think that at least something has to be going on.

The second thing is the boy in the dream. I feel as if I have met or seen him before, but I can't place where or when. I'm obsessed, trying to go through my memories and figure out where I recognize him from. I do this pretty much the entire fifty-minute ride to the airport. We finally arrive and they pull up to the United Airlines baggage drop-off area. Chris and Lea help me get my stuff out and place everything on the curb. After they're done, Chris gets back into the car, but Lea turns around to me and grabs me by the shoulders.

"Please figure out what's going on. Something tells me our dreams may have something to do with why you're going back to the states."

I simply nod my head, and she lets go. I know I can't really tell her anything, especially since I don't even know for sure if this is related to our dreams or not. I check in my luggage and make my way through security and then to my gate. As I sit down, there's a little girl there with her mom. She looks to be five years old. I don't really pay her any mind, but I start to realize that she has been staring at me the entire time. I soon realize that she is staring at me for a reason.

"I've seen you before," the little girl says to me.

I'm taken aback and confused, especially since I have never seen this girl before.

"Huh. Where did you see me at?" I assume she is going to say at security or coming into the airport.

Oh, how naïve I am to assume something normal is going to happen today.

"You were in my dream last night."

My stomach drops. I'm not in Chris and Lea's dreams, but they still have a connection to my dream from earlier. I don't want to know what the dream is about, but I know I need to gather this information so we can figure out what's going on. Her mother notices that she's talking to me and decides to tell me about the dream.

"I'm sorry she's bothering you. She did have a crazy dream last night, didn't you, Jordan?"

"Yes, I did. It was so scary."

"If you don't mind, ma'am, could you tell me about the dream?"

The mom switches seats with her daughter. "I'm Eden. What's your name?"

"I'm Dr. Koraline, a psychologist."

I don't usually introduce myself with the title, but I figure it might help ease the mother's suspicions about why I'm inquiring about the dream.

"Oh, wow. So today is my lucky day. Because I had no idea what to tell her what that dream meant." She looks relieved, but I'm nervous because I can't even explain my own dream.

She then proceeds to start telling me about Jordan's dream. I'm not certain why she doesn't allow her daughter to share the story; perhaps she wants to prevent her from becoming accustomed to speaking with strangers.

"My poor Jordan. She was out in the middle of nowhere on a flat grassy area as far as the eye could see. She said this woman whom she had never met before came up to her and told her she needed to get back to Kansas City to find the answers."

Kansas City? I stop listening at that point because that makes me very nervous. I used to work in Kansas City when I was still a psychiatrist. What is going on? Why are strangers having these subconscious connections to me?

I try to redirect my focus and get back to paying attention to her, but it's hard. I think I hear her talk a good bit about the environment Jordan was in and how vast it was. What brings me back in is when she gets to the part that was also in Chris and Lea's dream: the mysterious voice. This is what scares Jordan apparently. The voice says the exact same thing to her as it does to me and the others:

"DO NOT INTERFERE."

How am I supposed to take this? This just keeps adding to the mystery surrounding this whole dream situation. I'm not sure how to process it. I quickly get up and go to get coffee and purposely keep standing from a distance so someone can take my seat. I don't want to make it obvious that I'm trying to avoid sitting with Eden and Jordan. Once my former seat is taken, I find another and just put my headphones in and play on my phone until boarding starts.

Forty-five minutes pass, and they start the boarding process. I'm Priority, so I'm able to be one of the first ones in line. I really don't want to fall asleep on this flight. I'm terrified that I may have the same dream or another dream related to the first one. I'm not sure what to do because I already feel the coffee wearing off. I also don't want to drink coffee the whole flight.

I get to my seat in business class, which surprises me; the US government is paying for me to fly business class. I think it's generous of them, until I realize they may have only booked me in business because the flight is full. Go figure. Regardless, I'm thankful for the extra comfort on this flight. If nothing else, this is one decent thing to come from today.

It doesn't take long before we take off. As we ascend, I feel myself starting to drift. No. I can't. I don't want to fall asleep. However, my body is telling me otherwise. Maybe, just maybe, I won't have any more creepy dreams. My body is tired of me fighting it. I finally end up falling asleep.

The Second Dream

I find myself sitting in a rocking chair in the middle of a wheat field. I don't know exactly where I am, but it reminds me of the wheat fields I used to pass while driving through Kansas during my time living in Kansas City. So, I assume I must be somewhere in Kansas." I don't understand why I'm in the middle of a wheat field, or why I'm sitting in a rocking chair there. I look around, and there is wheat as far as I can see. The sky is an unusually vivid shade of blue, so bright it almost looks artificial. I have never seen it this blue before.

There's something about this dream that feels different. Every dream I've had so far has felt out-of-body, or the normal kind of dream where you just go along with it and don't know you're dreaming until you wake up. But in this one, I know. I don't know how I know, but I do. I wonder why I'm not on the plane, but then I realize… I'm dreaming. I even remember what happened in my previous dream, so I keep an eye out for the little boy and try to avoid the mysterious figure that spoke last time.

With all of this in mind, I just keep rocking away, not knowing at all what to expect. Thirty minutes pass, and out of nowhere, the little boy I saw in my previous dream appears. He just shows up when I look to my left. I stop rocking as he stands there, this time in a green onesie, staring at me. I decide I'll try to hold a conversation with him.

"You appeared in my last dream. Who are you?"

The boy doesn't say anything. He just continues standing there. I'm hoping he will eventually talk to me. We continue staring at each other for ten more minutes. It's quite awkward, honestly. I'm not sure what else to say. But unexpectedly, he breaks the silence.

"Why?" he asks quietly.

Confused, I ask for clarification. "Why… what?"

"Why… didn't you help me?"

Help him? My thoughts scatter as I try to figure out what he's talking about. Then I think about the first dream.

"If you're asking why I didn't help the last time, I did my best. I couldn't reach you due to the ground shaking so violently." I feel bad after saying that, thinking now that I should've done more to help.

"Not him. You can't stop him." His eyes are starting to well up.

"Then what are you talking about?" I'm even more confused at this point.

"Earlier. Why don't you help me earlier?" His head is now pointed towards the ground, and I can see tears dropping from his face.

I get out of the rocking chair to try and comfort him, but he backs up, not allowing me to get near him. I don't know what I did nor why he is like this. I don't have time to dwell on it because the trembling from the first dream has returned. This time, it's more violent. We both fall to the ground, but it doesn't last as long as the previous dream. I get back on my feet and look around. The vastness of wheat that surrounds us has now gone up in flames. There is fire everywhere!

However, it is not hot.

We are both confused but then a huge shadow comes over us from above. This means only one thing. I turn back and this time, I see a being. I can't make out what this being is. His entire body is black as night and the outline of his body looks like a monster out of a movie. His eyes are piercing red. I'm frozen in fear. I have no idea what to think or what to do. The boy starts wailing, and I grab him and hold him close. At least, I can try and protect him.

This creature, whatever it is, looks directly at us and he begins to snarl. The sound coming from its mouth is terrifying as its low growl makes me nervous. But the growl isn't what terrifies me; it's his teeth! He has very sharp teeth and he looks as if he's going to kill us! He quickly bends over and his face is right in front of ours. I feel an icy grip tighten around my chest, paralyzing me. My heart races, but my limbs refuse to respond; it's as if my body has turned to stone.

His teeth are still showing, and he is still growling! He then starts to speak.

"DO NOT MAKE ME TELL YOU AGAIN. DO NOT INTERFERE!"

He then attempts to go for us, opening his mouth and going in for the kill. We both scream and I wake up. I'm sweaty, catching my breath, and feeling dazed.

I didn't expect this dream to be as intense as it is! It takes me a bit to gather myself. I know that despite how bad this dream is, I need to write down everything that occurs so I can keep notes on everything. I know these dreams have to be connected to what's going on in the states. I go to the bathroom and get back to my seat to start writing down the details of the dream. While I'm doing this, I also write down some questions:

What does the boy mean I should've helped him earlier?

What is this creature?

What does his warning mean?

Is it possible that these dreams have real world implications outside of being connected to this project?

I really want to know the answers to these questions and figure out why and what's going on. I may not have time to investigate these questions immediately while I'm working on this project, but I intend to find the answers. I look to see how much time of the flight we have left. I didn't realize I've been asleep that long! There are only two hours left of this eight-hour flight! I did need the sleep. I play on my phone for a good bit until an announcement comes over the PA that takes me by surprise.

"Passengers and crew, this is the captain. We will not quite be landing in Washington just yet. We will be diverting to Philadelphia due to ATC issues at Washington. We will keep you updated as much as we can."

Well, this continues to be a long day.

Chapter 5

Mission Brief

I'll admit, I'm a bit frustrated about us having to be diverted. However, I don't think much of it. I can think of numerous flights I've been on that have been delayed or diverted for one reason or another. It isn't long before we begin our descent into Philadelphia. It is a clear night, and I can see the city lights as we descend. I check my phone. It's 12:30 AM here.

We eventually land and wait to disembark. As soon as I turn off airplane mode, I receive a text from the secretary asking me to call him once I get off the plane. It makes sense, I guess. I figure he probably wants to see when I arrive. Before we're let out, our pilot informs us that they will try to get us to DC in the morning. I make plans to stay at the airport and catch the flight so I don't have to go through security all over again.

I find a place at the gate lounge to get comfortable for the overnight and decide to text the secretary. I message him about us being diverted to Philadelphia and say that I'll be in DC in the morning, hopefully. Not long after he reads the message, he calls me.

"Hello?" I answer.

"Dr. Koraline, I have made arrangements for you to spend the night at the Delta Hotel, which is not too far from the airport. I'll come up and pick you up, and we will discuss things on the way to our next destination."

Meet me? Next destination? What is going on here?

"There's nothing for you to be worried about. I just need to meet with you in person as soon as possible so I can talk to you about the situation," he says.

I decide to ask him about our next "destination."

"When you say next destination, do you mean Washington?"

"I'll explain tomorrow. Get an Uber to your hotel and get some sleep, Dr. Koraline." He then ends the call.

I have a feeling I'm not going to Washington today. But if not there, then where? I'm not too happy that I'll be in the car with the secretary; however, I'm glad that I'll have the time I need to ask all the questions I want to ask. I start making my way to the front of the airport to get picked up and begin my Uber process. I didn't realize until now that since my plane was diverted, my luggage is probably not at baggage claim. Fortunately, I have enough stuff in my carry-on for the night. I'm not sure what I plan to do when I get to the hotel, but I know I'm probably not going to sleep. That dream was horrid, and I don't want to chance having another one like it, especially so soon after the last.

I finally make it to the pick-up area and find my Uber driver.

I arrive at my hotel, and what a welcoming sight it is. I'm so tired. After getting checked in and going to my room, I start thinking more about the dream I had on the flight, especially the part where the boy says I should've helped him earlier. I begin to

36

wonder if I know this boy from somewhere. He doesn't look super familiar to me, but I also wonder if we crossed paths sometime before these dreams. That would be the only way it would make sense for him to make that statement, but I really can't place whether I've seen or met him before.

I sit on my bed, wondering what's going to happen later on today. I wonder how the ride with the secretary will go and how many of my questions will get answered. I hope he at least confirms or refutes what British Intelligence has heard. Not long after I sit down, I receive a call from a masked number. I answer the call.

"This is Director Lynne. Please check the laptop." She then ends the call.

That's weird.

Fortunately, I place the laptop in my carry-on. After opening it and letting it boot up, a window from some kind of instant messaging program pops up on the screen.

It was from Director Lynne:

Dir_Lynne: We saw that your plane got diverted, is everything OK?

I attempt to connect the laptop to Wi-Fi but then realize it is already connected. I'm guessing the laptop is equipped with some type of satellite internet service. I hesitate, staring at the message. Something about Director Lynne still unsettles me. I can't tell if she is genuinely trying to help or if she has her own agenda. Still, the silence is starting to weigh on me. Maybe if I share what I know, she will fill in the gaps, or at least give me something to work with. I just hope I won't end up regretting it.

I respond.

Dr_Kor: As far as I know, everything is OK, they said there was ATC issues in Washington. However, I have the feeling that there's something more going on. Secretary Jones asked me to text him and he called right after getting my text. He informed me that I would be staying in Philadelphia and he will be coming up to pick me up and talk to me on the way to our next destination later in the day. I asked if the next destination was Washington, but he really didn't answer my question, so I'm assuming I'm not going to Washington later today.

It took a little bit for the director to respond.

Dir_Lynne: That is indeed weird, if we find out anything, we'll let you know. Thank you for keeping us in the loop.

Chat ended.

While I still don't like being in contact with British Intelligence, I hope they can find some answers about what's going on in Washington. So afterwards, I continue to focus on the dream that happens during the flight, at least as long as I can. I feel myself getting very sleepy, and I have the urge to sleep, but I'm very concerned about what I might dream next. Despite my worry, I end up falling asleep.

There is a knock at the door, which startles me awake. Looking through the peephole, I see it is Secretary Jones.

"Meet me at my car in twenty minutes. Look for the red Prius."

He then leaves, and I quickly start to get ready. I don't really have much to do besides brushing my teeth and my hair. There's no time for a shower. As I rush to get ready, it hits me: I cannot remember having any dreams last night. Maybe, just maybe, they are finally coming to an end.

After checking out, I find his car and get into the passenger seat. He looks really stressed. We pull out of the parking lot and begin making our way to the interstate.

"Dr. Koraline, I want to start by saying that I'm sorry for how all of this is being handled. However, we have had a huge national security issue come up, and we needed to bring you to the states."

"Mr. Secretary, why me? What was so important that you had to get me on a plane in the middle of the night?" I ask this with the knowledge I received from Director Lynne about other psychiatrists and psychologists being contacted as well.

"As we are not in a secure environment, I can't give you one hundred percent of the details yet. However, this is what I can tell you. About ten years ago, our government was contacted about a series of strange things happening in Kansas. There were no explanations for how or why these strange things were happening. We had no idea what was causing it, so we terminated the investigation. However, years later, we received a call from a psychiatrist in the area who said she had a patient, a boy, who claimed he had the ability to make people have nightmares when they were near him. Some researchers from the University of New Mexico and the University of Missouri decided to test this theory with the boy, and it turned out, despite how unbelievable it was, to be true."

My face turns white. I remember this case.

"This kid… I remember him. Well, not exactly him, but his sister. I was working as a psychiatrist in Kansas City at the time, and I received a referral to see his sister. She was complaining that her brother was giving her nightmares all the time. She couldn't explain it, and I couldn't get her to tell me what I thought was really going on. At that time, I assumed the nightmares were a codeword for something more serious, so I referred the case to Children's Services after eight sessions. That was one of my first cases after finishing school, and I remember feeling guilty about making the referral. Still, I genuinely believed something more was going on beneath the surface. A few years later, I began to reconsider the situation and wondered if he might have been telling the truth. Of course, this was purely hypothetical. I never truly believed it was possible. That case is what led me to dive deeper into dreams and the subconscious. But as time passed, I completely forgot about him," I say, letting everything spill out.

I start to wonder if the boy in the dreams is the same boy from all those years ago, but I don't recall what he looks like. I only saw his sister, and I don't know what happened to her.

"Yes, Dr. Koraline, we're very familiar with what took place. We thoroughly researched his history when he came into our care, so we had you on standby when things started getting interesting a couple of years ago." Secretary Jones is about to say more, but I cut him off.

"What happened to him before he was in the government's care? I just figured he went into foster care, maybe, and hopefully was able to go back home after they figured out this whole scenario with the nightmares," I say with a very guilty conscience.

"After your report was sent, the state took it into strong consideration, and they removed both of them from the home. His sister was removed too, in case the environment would cause additional trauma. It was a very messy situation. The sister was able to return home. However, he did not do well in many of the homes where he was placed. He struggled to remain in a single foster home because his frequent strange dreams were unnerving the foster parents. It wasn't until he ended up in the foster home of a psychiatrist who decided to look more deeply into his dreams. At

40

first, she didn't believe him. But one night, she ended up having a dream that was exactly the one he said she would have. This continued for several weeks until she decided to contact another psychiatrist for help. Despite months of research and consulting with colleagues, she was about to give up until strange things started happening around the town. During this time, children services discovered that the government was trying to search for answers. They reached out to us and asked for our assistance."

This is overwhelming. I don't really know how to make sense of it all. More than anything, I feel a heavy sense of guilt. I had no idea that referring this boy to foster care would set off a chain of events that caused him so many years of hardship. Then I think to myself, what was I supposed to do? I had no reason to trust what he claimed. But what if I had? I don't know exactly what I would've done. However, I believe I did the right thing at the time with the knowledge that I had. At this point, I'm scared to ask any more questions. But I know I have to.

"What was the boy's name? This case was at the beginning of my career, so I can't remember his name. Also, what kind of research was done on him? He wasn't tortured or anything, was he?"

"His name is Cody, and I assure you that he was not tortured. We had him stay at a foster home near the facility where we were conducting research. It was just a lot of sleep and us monitoring activity. This took place for the first three years of research on him. However, we had a situation arise, and we needed to relocate him immediately. He is now in Richmond, Virginia for the time being."

"What happened that he needed to be moved?" I ask, trying to piece the puzzle together. I'm curious if there is a connection between why he was moved and what is going on in Washington.

"I'm not at liberty to tell you. I know that seems unfair, but we are still trying to figure it out ourselves."

What is that supposed to mean? I don't know if he really cannot tell me, or if he's purposely withholding information.

I decide to move on from that for now and ask about the current situation. "Does he have the same arrangement as he did in the previous place?"

"Unfortunately, he does not. Instead of being placed with a family, he is now staying at the facility where we are conducting research. This was done for the safety of the public." Secretary Jones seems determined not to give me more information than this.

How bad is the situation if they must keep Cody away from the public? If that's the case, then Secretary Jones should give me far more information than he is letting on. I must ask him more questions. I need as much information as possible if they want me to assist in any way. If I don't get the answers I need, I may have no choice but to rely on British Intelligence. I really do not like that option. I'm not a fan of either government trying to get what they want out of me. What I do know is that I have to do whatever it takes to get the answers I need. So, if I must rely on British Intelligence, then that is what I will do.

For now, though, I will continue to ask. "I've only had contact with his sister. What exactly are you expecting from me? It seems like I've had the least amount of contact with him."

Secretary Jones stares at the road, his expression tight and reluctant, like he's dreading the response before it even begins.

"We didn't have plans to contact you, though we have you on the standby list. That all changed a couple of weeks ago. Anyone who has been in contact with him experienced dreams that he controls in one way or another until a couple of weeks ago. Those working with him have recently begun experiencing certain elements of the new nightmares he's been having. While the specific details vary from person to person, one thing remains the same in every dream—you. You appear in all of them. When we asked Cody if he could explain it, he said he couldn't. These dreams are beginning to impact people in ways we've never encountered before. There are more elements to the dream, but again, I cannot tell you at this time what they are."

I sit in silence for five minutes as I try to wrap my mind around this. I never think that a case I had from ten years ago, one I barely worked on, is now going to have an impact on my life.

"So, you bring me out here to figure out why I'm in his dreams and in the dreams of those around him?"

"Yes, Dr. Koraline. We need your help."

"Okay, it's strange; I'll give you that. But how does that make it a national security threat? And if it really is that serious, why are you coming to me instead of going through the usual channels?"

"Doctor, if I could tell you, I would. But at this time, it is in your best interest to hear it in a secure facility."

Blocked again. I don't want to wait that long. My whole life gets disrupted for this. I would think I'm owed a full explanation as to why. Why does it have to be told in a secured facility? Is he concerned about phones listening in or bugs in his car? Then my stomach starts to sink. Could he possibly know about the laptop I get from Director Lynne? I hope not. If they find out about that laptop, I'm done. I'll be arrested for sure. Pushing aside the panic, I decide to ask some more personal questions about Cody.

"I believe Cody is six around the time I send him into foster care. Is that correct?"

"Yes, it is. He's not a little boy anymore. I encourage you not to blame yourself for what happened, Doctor. You didn't know what you were dealing with," he responds.

I appreciate him trying to help me, but it still doesn't ease my guilty conscience.

"I understand. Could you at least answer me about where we are going? I'm assuming we're going to Richmond?" I ask.

"Yes, we are. The facility we are going to is right outside of Richmond," answers Secretary Jones.

I'm glad to know where I'm going. With some distance still remaining before we reach Richmond, I retrieve my phone and occupy myself with it. I notice a text from Director Lynne telling me to check my laptop when I get a chance. I'm curious what she wants to talk to me about. I'm at least hoping that she finds some answers to the questions Secretary Jones keeps refusing to answer. If I can pull together what they have already said and what they might still reveal, I might be able to start filling in the gaps and get closer to the truth. I'll have a better idea once I get a moment alone to check the laptop.

While I think about that and play on my phone, I realize we're not on the interstate anymore. I didn't notice when we took an exit. I open Maps on my phone to see where we are, and I see that we're in Maryland, about thirty miles west of Baltimore. I want to ask why we are taking the detour, but I figure I'll get the usual "I can't tell you" answer. I draw my own conclusion: something really must be going on in Washington, and he's trying to avoid me seeing or picking up on what's happening. So, I don't know if we're going to take back roads the rest of the way or if we're eventually going to get back on the interstate.

Regardless, this makes the trip even longer, and I start falling asleep. As usual, I'm terrified of what I might dream, especially since I'm in the car with the secretary and I'm concerned he may try to extract additional information from me. I'm not scared that he'll hurt me, but I don't trust his intentions since I'm still in the dark. The jet lag is relentless, and no matter how hard I try to stay awake, my body just gives out. Once again, I slip into sleep without meaning to.

Chapter 6

Past Mistakes

The Third Dream

Given the two previous dreams I've had, I expect to find myself in another strange setting: isolated, with only that boy for company. But this dream turns out differently. I find myself in a very unexpected place: my old office in Kansas City. This is my first office of my own after finishing my master's in psychology, years of interning, and the crazy process of getting licensed. There's no one in the office, so I decide to look around just to reminisce. I glance at my desk and notice that my desktop is already logged in. I want to see what date it is: September 14, 2013. I see that I'm at the very beginning of my time working in Kansas City. I officially opened my office on July 26th of that year. Behind my desk, I have my two degrees posted, my bachelor's and master's; I haven't started on my doctorate yet. I continue to look around and see the brown wood paneling walls that I would eventually get rid of and have redone. I hated those walls.

I think back to how I ended up in Kansas City. I wanted to work in my home state of Georgia, but I was presented with an opportunity to use the office of a mentor of mine who was retiring. I feel like this is an opportunity I can't turn down, so I move to Kansas and begin preparing to practice there. I've never been to his office. I met with him numerous times in school and at conventions that I've attended. So, when he first tells me about his office and where he runs his practice, I assume it's Kansas City, Missouri. I find out after getting the paperwork that it's in the Kansas part of the city. Having never gone to Kansas before, I'm a little bummed at the prospect. I've heard there's pretty much nothing in the state. At least I can always go to the Missouri side, and I did quite often. Though I sometimes enjoy the Kansas side for different reasons.

While I'm reminiscing, I hear the door being unlocked and opened. It's me coming into work. Well, my old self at least. She can't see me though. It's like I'm a ghost and I'm just here to observe. That's when it strikes me. I snap out of my reminiscing and recognize that I have to focus. My recent dreams have been trying to convey something, yet their meaning remains elusive. I hope that this dream might finally reveal the answers to the lingering questions left unresolved in the previous ones. I'm also hoping that maybe in this dream I can find some answers to the secretary's questions. One thing I've noticed is that these dreams keep getting weirder. While I'm in the dream, I seem to know that I'm riding in the car and that I'm hoping to find answers before we arrive in Richmond. While I'm glad that I'm self-aware, it's making me freak out a little bit, knowing that I have this amount of awareness in my dreams.

I know I need to use this to my advantage. I go into observation mode and just stand off to the side and watch myself work. It's weird, watching myself. It's even more weird seeing how much younger I looked back then. I also didn't realize how nervous I was. I don't notice until a few years ago that I have anxiety tics. What is it about this date that is important to everything that's going on? A part of me starts to think that it might be the day that I get the referral for Cody's sister, which would make the most sense, considering what I was just told in the car. While I'm thinking, I'm startled when my assistant Becky comes into the office.

"Geneva, you have an emergency referral from Shawnee in Johnson County."

Hearing her talk, I didn't realize how much I've missed people calling me by my first name, Geneva. I don't hear it often because everyone calls me Dr. Koraline.

My old self looks up at Becky with a searching look. "Emergency referral? What details do we have?"

"It's a unique one for sure. An eight-year-old girl is claiming that her brother is giving her nightmares. The parents were dismissive of the claims, but they noticed that she was getting more and more distressed every day, and they're concerned that something might be going on. They tried to get their son to talk, but he simply says he doesn't know why it's happening and that he can't control it. They've been consulting child psychiatrists in hopes of gathering insights from their daughter and clues that might shed light on the situation. So far, they've had no luck. The parents are also counting on your fresh perspective, believing that, as a new psychiatrist, you might offer answers they haven't found elsewhere."

I admit, it's a bit crazy seeing my facial expressions when Becky tells me about the referral. My younger self is in a bit of shock and disbelief. I forget how dismissive I was about the whole thing. I feel bad that I was that dismissive about it.

"That is unique, to say the least. How much do you want to bet that the brother is guilty of doing something that the parents don't know and the sister is covering for him?"

I'm appalled by how unprofessional I was when I first started out. I know better than to come up with a definitive judgment before hearing the client first. However, this case is so unique. It's very weird. There's no logical explanation to these dreams, other than them being covers or codewords for something else.

Knowing what I know now, I wish I could go back in time and fix this. I start to think about what would've happened if I'd requested to see her brother too and see for myself what was happening with him. There are no words to describe the shame I feel watching this take place all over again.

"You're probably right, Geneva. Do you want to accept it? It sounds like they really have little options left."

"Of course!" I say without hesitation. "I'll see what I can do with the sister, but if they've already gone to so many other people, I don't see the harm in doing more than eight sessions. That's my guess at least. We shall see. What's the sister's name?"

I can't believe how fast I want to get through with these sessions and I don't even have her scheduled yet!

"Ashley Thomas," Becky responds.

"Okay, let's put her down to begin next Tuesday. Will the parents be a part of the sessions?"

"No. They've been in previous sessions with other psychiatrists, but they're trying a new approach and hoping that Ashley would be willing to tell more details if she wasn't in the presence of her parents," says Becky. "You'll have time to prepare for it later. We have a consultation we need to get to."

My dream self and Becky leave the office. I recall holding consultations in a smaller room within the practice. I decide to go and sit in my old chair and think about everything that just took place. Given how indifferent I was toward her brother, it wouldn't shock me if he harbors some resentment toward me. A well-deserved grudge. I'm not sure what I'm going to do, but before I can even think, Becky comes back into the office and she does something I don't expect.

"Geneva, your next appointment is here."

She can see me? How? I thought this entire dream was a flashback but now I'm a part of it? I decide to go with it and ask her who is next to be seen.

"Becky, I'm having some trouble remembering. If you don't mind, could you tell me who my next client is?" I ask.

"This appointment just came up. His name is Cody Thomas. And he needs to talk to you urgently."

It's him. The boy I send away without truly grasping his situation. I was hoping to avoid facing him until I reach Richmond, wanting to use the drive to steady my nerves. But maybe confronting him now will help me regain my composure before I get there. Regardless, I know there is only one thing to do.

"Bring him in," I reply.

I'm not ready for this, but honestly, I don't think I'm ever going to be fully ready. Becky brings him in and, to my shock, it's the same boy who has been showing up in my dreams. Deep down, I've suspected all along that Cody might be the boy I kept seeing, and now I'm nearly certain. He's wearing a brown onesie, the same type of clothing that always shows up in these dreams, not just mine but in others' accounts too. While I can't say with absolute certainty that Cody is the boy from every dream, the likelihood keeps growing. He takes a seat in one of the large brown leather chairs across from my desk and begins to speak.

"Dr. Koraline, I really wish that you had spoken to me. I would've been able to show you what I can do. No one believes me, no matter how many times I've tried to explain it to them."

"Cody, I can't make up for what I did in the past. What I did was inexcusable, even if I didn't believe that you were giving your sister nightmares. All I can say is that I'm sorry."

Cody looks away for a few minutes and then speaks again. "I've had plenty of time to think on what you did and I've forgiven you. It's been years. Now I'm giving you a chance to ask me some questions and do the session that you didn't do ten years ago."

I'm extremely grateful that he's willing to let me ask him questions, even though I messed up.

"Cody, as much as I want to start off by asking about the current things that are taking place, let's talk about ten years ago. Why did you give your sister nightmares?"

"I wasn't trying to make it happen; it just did. I would have the dream first, then tell my sister about it, and later that night she would have the same dream. I thought it was strange when, the next day, she described almost the exact same dream I had; only hers was even scarier. But then I started to think that I really might have been giving my sister these dreams. I don't know how to explain it, and no one has figured out why. Then, within the next two years, people around me started to have the dreams that I had had the night before. Most of them were nightmares. I can count on one hand how many nice dreams I've had."

I feel sorry for him. That is a heavy burden for a person, let alone a kid, to carry. However, I find this intriguing. How is this happening? I'm not going to pretend that I understand how this is taking place, but maybe I can get to the root cause of these nightmares.

"I see. When did these dreams start?"

I now try to make attempts to discover the trigger and see if we can figure out a way for him to cope. Perhaps if we can do this, the dreams will stop.

Cody has to think about when it starts. He finally comes up with an answer.

"It started three months before my sister came to see you. If you're trying to figure out if something happened then, I really can't think of anything. Life was normal."

Well, that's a bust. Unless he's trying to hide something, I'm at a loss at how and why he starts having these nightmares. Before I can ask any more questions, I hear someone coming.

"I think we're out of time. But please, hold on to this." He quickly reaches into his pocket and hands me a key. I grab the key, and I put it in my pocket, but when I look up, he is gone. That's weird, but this is a dream after all. I get up from the chair and stand by the wall. The door opens and I think that it's either myself or Becky. Unfortunately, I turn out to be wrong. I hear the recognizable growl and I fear the worst. I guess I can't have one without the other: the boy and the creature. However, the creature

52

looks different than in my previous dream. This time, he looks more like a man, but he has red eyes and a trench coat. It is still weird because his whole body and the trench coat are completely black.

He begins to speak, "You have continued to interfere. Now the day is near!"

What is happening? What kind of threat is this? Was this a threat against me or Cody? Or was this a broader threat? I decide I would attempt to talk to him, or it, whatever he was.

"What do you mean 'the day is near?'"

He shows his teeth, which are still scary, just like in the previous dream, and says, "You will find out soon." He then leaves, and I wake up.

I need to find answers now!

Chapter 7

What's with the keys?

A wave of panic washes over me. I'm sweating and struggling to catch my breath. I glance outside and see that we're still on the road, the scenery rushing past in a blur. For a moment, I worry that Secretary Jones might be watching me, wondering what is wrong. But he seems focused on driving, minding his own business. Hopefully, he will not decide to ask about it later. I do find it odd that he doesn't ask any questions. I begin to realize that I have been asleep longer than anticipated. We are already almost to Richmond. I'm not sure how long the secretary is going to stay when he drops me off, but I do need to ask him a question before he leaves.

"Will someone retrieve my luggage? It's still on its way to DC."

"Don't worry, Doctor, we are already working on that," he responds.

I hope he is telling the truth, because I really need my stuff.

"Here is the plan, Doctor. You'll be staying at a hotel in Bellwood, and you'll be assigned a personal assistant who is responsible for your transportation. Her name is Melanie Moon, and she'll meet you at your hotel an hour after I drop you off."

Melanie Moon. That's an interesting last name. I'm curious about it. She sounds nice. I hope she is, at least.

The secretary continues, "Here is a badge for you to use to enter the facility. It's located in an office space right outside the city limits of Richmond. We are trying to stay as conspicuous as possible; we don't want to attract the wrong kind of attention."

He hands me a badge that has my official picture from the university on it, my name, and a random sequence of numbers. It also says "Department of Homeland Security" at the bottom. I go ahead and put it in my pocket, but I realize that something else is in my pocket that wasn't there before. I pull it out and it's the key that I received in the dream! Normally, I would be questioning how any of this is even possible, but at this point, I have chosen to set aside most of my assumptions about reality. I return the key to my pocket in a hurry, careful not to let the secretary notice. I will focus on the key later. My main goal is to get into my hotel room and try to contact Director Lynne while I have time.

It does not take much longer for us to get to my hotel, and I go ahead and start working on getting my stuff out of the car after he gets my hotel key.

"Okay, Doctor, I'll not be in much contact with you for a while. I'll try to get the rest of the information to you. The staff inside will provide some additional details, but I'll provide the rest of the information when I can."

"Thank you," I reply.

"Also, your luggage should be dropped off to you tonight," says Secretary Jones.

"Thank you. I do appreciate it."

He then drives off in a bit of a hurry. I wonder if he's rushing to get back to Washington to address whatever is going on. Maybe I can ask Director Lynne if she knows what is going on there. Once I get in my room, I use the bathroom and then I quickly get out the laptop. As before, I see I have a message on that instant messaging program.

Dir_Lynne: I'm not sure what all you were told by the secretary, but this is what we have found out so far. For some reason, this project revolves around a kid by the name of Cody, who has the ability to manipulate dreams. We're not sure how accurate this information is because this seems really strange, but we do know that he is currently being held at a facility in Richmond, Virginia. Before that, he was at a facility and foster home in Socorro, New Mexico. We are not sure why he was in Socorro or why they picked that location, but that's where the bulk of the research on him was done. Then, out of the blue, he was quickly taken to the facility in Richmond. We have no details as to why he was taken away from Socorro, but from what we have gathered from inside sources, it was an unexpected and urgent move.

Huh. That is concerning that they felt the need to move him so urgently. I wonder what the issue was and why the secretary couldn't have told me this information. I'm assuming that he's concerned that I would try to figure out what's going on.

Dr_Kor: I was told about Cody and was given some background information about him. It turns out I do have a connection to him. Years ago, I saw his sister in a session when I worked in Kansas City. She complained that her brother was giving her nightmares. Since the way she was explaining this to me didn't make any sense, and I initially assumed that the term 'nightmares' implied something nefarious or was a code word for something else,

I contacted children services. This is a big reason why I have been contacted and my involvement has been requested, or rather, demanded.

I don't want to say more than that about Cody, since I was mainly trying to get information instead of giving it.

Dir_Lynne: That makes sense. We're currently trying to piece together what happened in New Mexico that led to Cody being relocated. We've also been working to gather more information about the situation in DC, but so far, details have been scarce. Flights have resumed into the two main Washington airports, but we've noticed that planes are avoiding the immediate DC area. The only official explanation we've been given is that there's some sort of interference affecting communication systems around the capital. We're actively monitoring chat to see if this type of interference is happening elsewhere in the country or globally. We'll continue to keep you updated as best we can, though the situation is still developing and we're having to sort through a large amount of incoming intelligence.

Dr_Kor: OK, thank you.

Chat ended

I'm curious about what happened in Socorro. I have a feeling that the key to this whole thing might be in Socorro or somewhere nearby. The situation in DC is sounding more suspicious than I previously thought. I check some news outlets to see if anything is being reported about what's going on in DC. Much to my surprise, there's barely any coverage on it. I find an article from the Washington Post that says officials have no comment about the entire situation. So, the public doesn't seem to know what's really happening.

I hop over to some social media sites to check if anyone in the DC area is posting about it. Aside from a few complaints about bad cell service, there's nothing out of the ordinary. I'll check again later today to see if any new posts come up. I have a strong feeling there's a coordinated effort to keep the whole situation under wraps.

I'm not sure how I plan to spend the rest of the hour while I wait, but then there's a knock at the door. I wonder if the secretary is coming back because he forgot to tell me something. I open the door, but it isn't the secretary. It's a woman I don't recognize. She has a fair complexion with warm undertones, suggesting a mixed heritage. Her green eyes meet mine, and her dark brown hair is tied back in a ponytail. She's wearing a red button-up shirt and black jeans.

"Dr. Koraline, I'm Melanie, your assistant. Please forgive me for showing up early, but there's a situation happening at the facility, and they've asked me to pick you up right away."

"What's going on?" I ask.

"I'm not sure. I was out getting coffee when Dr. Hamilton told me to bring you in as soon as possible. He sounded very stressed on the phone," Melanie says.

"That's probably not a good sign. I'm ready, so let's get going," I reply with urgency.

I'm not sure I'm ready to walk into whatever is happening over there, but it looks like I'll be hitting the ground running. Melanie drives quickly but carefully to the facility. It's only about a ten-minute drive, so we're not in the car for long. She stays quiet for most of the trip, and I don't know what to say either. Everything is moving so fast that it's hard to keep up. I feel overwhelmed, still trying to process what's happening.

We pull into a small parking lot; this building is smaller than I expected. I think I've seen houses that are bigger than this place.

We both get out of the car, and I follow Melanie as she leads the way inside. The lobby is small and dimly lit. A lone man is behind the front desk, his eyes locked on the entrance like he's been waiting for us. The moment he sees us, he jumps up with nervous urgency. His posture is tense, not afraid, but ready.

"Quickly now," he says, motioning toward the scanner. "Scan your badges and get in there. No time to lose!"

We scan our badges and quickly go through the door. We enter a narrow hallway, the walls seeming to close in around us, heavy with an eerie, oppressive silence. However, the silence does not last long. We begin to hear screaming. Just a few feet to our right is a door, shut tight but doing nothing to muffle the horrific sound pouring out. Screams fill the air, raw and desperate, each one laced with pain and panic.

The screaming alone is enough to freeze us in place, dread crawling over my skin. We move closer, but fear grips us and holds us at the threshold. Slowly, we lean forward and look inside. We don't know what we are about to see, but it's clear we are not ready for it.

There's Cody, slumped in a chair, his screams echoing through the room. A man, flanked by three others, hovers nearby, all of them trying in vain to calm him down.

"What are y'all doing to him?" I yell to one of the staffers.

"Doctor, you have to believe me, this has never happened before! We don't know what's going on!" he replies.

No matter what they do, they can't get Cody to stop screaming. I'm not sure what to do, but I have the feeling that they are waiting for me to try something. So, I take a gamble and decide to go near him.

"Cody," I say to him, softly and nervously. "What's wrong?"

Cody does not respond. He continues to scream for another minute, and then all of a sudden, he stops. He opens his eyes, revealing his pupils; an unnatural and vivid red. I have no idea what's happening right now. I'm freaking out, but I try to hide it from the others. However, something about his eyes catches my attention. They look very familiar. They look exactly the same as the figure that approached me in the dream. Cody then looks straight at me and begins to speak.

"This… is the beginning of the end."

He then closes his eyes and becomes unconscious. I don't know what to think. There is only silence as everyone tries to process what they have just witnessed. The only conclusion I can reach is that the figure from my previous dream is speaking through Cody. If it's truly controlling him like a puppet, then the warning it delivered is even more ominous than before. One thing is clear: I need to talk to the researchers about my dreams sooner rather than later.

The man I spoke to when I first entered the room starts talking.

"This is a first for us. We've never seen him act this way, nor have we ever seen his eyes do that before," he says nervously.

I look at his badge and see that his name is Dr. James Hamilton.

"Doctor, you must've triggered something within him by coming here," he continues.

Even though I already expected this outcome, his statement confirms that they'll be turning to me for answers. I'm hoping he will tell me something, but it looks like we are all on the same page when it comes to information.

"Are you familiar with my past with him and his family?" I ask.

"Y-y-yes…" Dr. Hamilton says, still trembling from what he just saw. "I'm not sure what set off his screaming, but it does seem like the entire episode was somehow triggered by your presence in the area. We just don't know the reason yet. I'm hoping you can provide some insight to us."

I then proceed to tell him and everyone else in the room about the dreams I've had. I go into as much detail as I can remember, hoping that maybe they can tell me something that will make sense of all this. After I finish, everyone in the room is looking at me, wide-eyed.

"I… don't know what to say," Dr. Hamilton says.

"What do you know? There has to be an explanation to this. You all have been researching him longer than I have," I say to Dr. Hamilton.

Melanie interjects, "We've been at a standstill. We're hoping that you can provide us with some information. Plus, we aren't told what happened when he was researched in New Mexico."

"Hold on, none of you were in New Mexico with him?" I ask, shocked at what I was just told.

Dr. Hamilton responds, "Correct. We were brought in and given very little information about what was discovered about Cody beforehand. We have made numerous attempts to find out what exactly happened there, but Homeland Security refuses to give us the information,"

One of my worst fears becomes reality. Secretary Jones is probably not going to give me the information anytime soon. Looks like I'm going to have to rely solely on British Intelligence after all.

"If you don't have full access to what was researched in New Mexico, then what is your objective?" I ask.

None of it makes sense. I can't wrap my head around what they are trying to accomplish.

"We're tasked with investigating the nature of Cody's ability to project his dreams into the environment and occasionally trigger dream states in others. Our early theories explore possibilities like abnormal brainwave resonance, heightened neural connectivity, and unknown forms of cognitive transmission. So far, none of these theories hold up under scrutiny. The phenomenon appears to operate beyond the boundaries of current neuroscience and psychology, perhaps touching on fields we have yet to fully discover or define. Every time we believe we're close to understanding it, unforeseen variables emerge and unravel our progress, forcing us to return to the beginning and question everything once more," says Dr. Hamilton.

"Complicating matters further, Homeland Security assigns us to this project under the expectation that personnel based in New Mexico would provide a full briefing. We're told to expect communication within two weeks. That was six months ago. Since then, Washington goes silent. No updates. No explanations. Just Cody, and the questions that keep multiplying." Melanie says frustratingly.

"According to the secretary, weird things were happening around the town that Cody was living in, which prompts him to be taken to be studied and researched," I say.

"That's one of the things that we have considered, and we still have it on the table as a possibility. However, it's hard to confirm anything without Washington giving us the full story," says Melanie angrily.

I know they expect me to stay at the facility for a little while and assist with research as much as I can, but I hope they allow me to return to my hotel room for the rest of the day. I need to get in contact with London and see if they can help me start digging for information.

"As much as I would like to stay longer, review the information you've gathered, and offer any help I can, I would prefer to observe him when he's in a more stable condition. Would it be too much to ask if I return to my hotel room and begin looking into a few things to prepare for tomorrow? Hopefully, he will be in a better state by then," I ask.

Dr. Hamilton gives me a blank stare; I can tell he doesn't like my request. "If you insist. But you need to return here at 5 AM sharp tomorrow morning."

"I will, Dr. Hamilton. There's just a lot I need to process, and I'd like to try to get myself in the right frame of mind before I interact with Cody more." I try to come up with the best excuse I can, though it can be argued that it is true.

"Do what you need to do, Doctor." He and the other assistants who are in the room with him make their way out, their footsteps fading down the hall. It is just Melanie and me now.

Everything is happening so fast, I barely have time to take in the room. It looks like a bedroom of sorts, with Cody lying in a bed at the center. To my right, I notice a large window. But it's impossible to see through. I assume it's a two-way mirror, likely for Dr. Hamilton and the others to observe him.

Melanie gently taps my shoulder. "Are you ready to go?"

"Yes."

She leads me out of the building and back into her car. The drive to the hotel is quiet, which I appreciate. I'm not in the mood to talk. We pull up to the hotel, and as I'm getting out, Melanie stops me.

"Just so you know, Dr. Hamilton has been stressing out about this since day one. He really is expecting you to provide as many answers as possible. I just want to give you a heads up to let you know how intense it's going to be over the coming days. If you need anything, just shoot me a text."

"Thanks, Melanie. You have a good rest of the day."

"You, too."

As soon as I get out of the car, I walk quickly to my room. As I approach the door, a loud beeping sound catches my attention from inside the room. My nerves kick in. I have no idea what's causing the sound. I start to hesitate, but I go into my room anyway. I'm relieved to see that it's just the laptop I received from Director Lynne. It does unnerve me, however, since the laptop has never made that sound before. I open it up and see that the noise is a message notification from the chat program. What catches my attention is the fact that I have an unread message from Director Lynne and another from someone I don't recognize. The sender reads, "Gary."

I open the message from Director Lynne first:

Dir_Lynne: You should be receiving a message from someone who wants to meet with you and share some information. He's not part of our team, but we did our best to vet him with the resources we had. He met enough of our criteria that we felt it was worth allowing him to reach out. Hopefully, he'll be able to provide you with something useful.

I then open the message from "Gary."

Gary: Meet me at hotel room 108. I have dinner and information for you.

I'm in room 215, so I have to head back downstairs. I make my way toward his room, feeling a growing tension with every step. Normally, I would have serious reservations about meeting a complete stranger, but time feels like it's slipping through my fingers. I need more information, and I need it now. When I reach his door, I just stand there, frozen. I can hardly believe what I'm doing or how everything has led up to this point. Here I am, about to turn to Gary, someone I've never met, for answers. Then again, if I'm being honest, everyone I've crossed paths with in the past twenty-four hours has been a stranger. Yet, this feels even riskier. I have no idea how this is going to unfold, and that uncertainty is hitting me harder than I expect.

"Well, here goes nothing," I say to myself. I gently knock on the door and nervously await his response.

Chapter 8

Turn Down the Noise

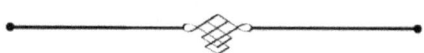

T he door opens slowly. The room is barely lit, shadows stretching across the walls. Maybe it's the dimness, or maybe something else, but an uneasy feeling settles over me.

"Come in quickly!" he says in a whisper.

Every fiber of my being does not want to go into that room, but I know I must. I go in and he pulls out the chair from the desk for me to sit. He looks worn down, like he hasn't slept in days. His short brown hair is messy, and his hazel eyes are bloodshot and tired. His skin is a little darker than mine, with a tan that seems more artificial than natural.

"We will talk and eat," Gary says in a hushed tone.

He takes out food from a bag labeled Old Highway Diner, a simple cheeseburger with fries and a drink. He also has the same thing. He hands me my food and then grabs his and sits down across from me on his bed. We both begin to eat, and he starts to talk.

"I know it's been a rough journey for you. I'm sorry that you had to get dragged into this mess with hardly any information. I'm not going to tell you my actual name; you can just keep calling me Gary for now."

"Thanks for dinner, Gary. To be honest, I'm not sure where to even start. Tell me what you can about yourself and why there's so much secrecy around this project."

I don't want to push too hard. It looks like he has had it way worse than I have.

"I was an assistant helping researchers with Cody in New Mexico."

Finally, I may have someone who can give me some information on what went down!

He continues, "I'm here to tell you some information that I know the government has not shared with you. There's a reason why they are trying to keep this covered up."

"What happened? This sounds very serious and concerning."

He stops eating. "I was on the project the entire time in New Mexico. For two years, Cody's dream-related abilities were puzzling but contained. He adjusted well to his foster family, and things felt under control. But that all changed six months ago."

"What occurred six months ago?" I realize as soon as that question leaves my lips that he is probably in the process of answering it. I let my impatience get the best of me.

"It all started with a package. There was nothing special about the package; where it was delivered to was the issue. For some reason, the package ends up at a store in Magdalena, about thirty miles west of Socorro. An aid who's in charge of picking up Cody from his foster home and bringing him to the facility is asked to go and retrieve the package. She takes Cody with her without permission, violating protocol. The research managers believe she hasn't picked him up yet, and she fails to inform them otherwise. She starts her drive to Magdalena, but she gets too distracted with her phone because her service isn't working well and she's trying to get maps back online." He stops and takes a couple more bites of food.

I try to be patient, to show some compassion and let him finish eating, but it's difficult. I want to know what happens next.

He finally starts back up after he sips on his soda. "Since she's messing with her phone and her signal isn't reliable, she drives right past Magdalena. She drives an additional thirty-five miles before she realizes her mistake, and she ends up in the very small town of Datil. She panics and tries to call her supervisor, but she doesn't have any service. So, she stops at a gas station and asks one of the employees for directions. She leaves Cody in the car by himself. The employee informs her that she's way out of the way and needs to go back the direction she came from. When she returns to the car, Cody starts complaining about a headache. So, the aid goes back inside and purchases him a bottle of water and they start making their way back to Magdalena. When they're about twenty-five miles east of Datil, Cody's headache intensifies into a migraine, and he starts to scream. The aid panics and pulls over and tries to comfort him, but to no avail. She then desperately tries to call her supervisor but her service is still spotty. She decides to rush to Magdalena as fast as possible in the hopes of getting at least a little bit of service. Once she's in town, she stops at a store and is able to call her supervisor. She notices that she has multiple missed calls due to the foster mom contacting the researchers because she had forgotten to give him his lunch before he was picked up. She initially tries to call the aid, but it kept going straight to voicemail, due to her not having service. Her supervisor is very angry that she has taken him on this errand without permission, but it turns to concern as he hears him screaming in the background. His screaming is so loud that store employees call the police. Her supervisor, along with a few other researchers, arrive at the same time as the sheriff's department. They try to explain to the police why they are there, and why their involvement isn't needed, but the police aren't budging. Cody continues to scream, and then he stops."

He starts to breathe a bit heavily after he stops talking. I'm hoping he can tell me why Cody is screaming. He finishes a couple more bites, gets some of his drink, and gets back to talking.

"The research managers were able to convince the police to leave. They take Cody back to Socorro and the aid follows them back to the facility. The aid is severely reprimanded and interrogated about what happened. They are convinced that the aid did something to him. She swears up and down that she didn't. Since they aren't getting the answers they want, she is stripped of most of her responsibilities, and she continues to be interrogated. The researchers run tests on Cody, but they don't see anything that would cause him to act the way he did. A week passes and nothing out of the ordinary occurs. The aid is on the verge of being fired until she comes running into the facility and asks to speak to the project managers. She is having coffee with a friend at a local coffee shop who works at New Mexico Tech in town. She discloses that the friend is frustrated because there is something going on with the equipment that he supervises and he has no idea how it started."

"Equipment? What equipment?" I ask.

"The VLA."

I give him a confused face. "The VLA? What is that?"

"The VLA, or the 'Very Large Array,' is one of the most powerful tools we have for studying space. It's made up of twenty-seven huge radio dishes, each as big as a house, spread out over a large area outside of Magdalena. The VLA uses radio waves, like a giant set of ears listening to space. It helps scientists study distant stars, black holes, and even entire galaxies by picking up signals we can't see with our eyes."

I'm even more confused. I now understand what the VLA is, but I don't see how it's relevant to my situation.

He continues before I can ask any more questions. "I know that you're probably asking yourself, what does this have to do with Cody? Here's the connection: the aid's friend informs her that all of these issues start a week ago, around the very same time that she accidentally drives to and from Datil. When you drive to Datil, you pass the VLA; you can't miss it."

He stops to continue eating. I start eating again too because I realize I've barely touched my dinner. We both eventually finish our dinners, and I take the opportunity to ask a question.

"So, what exactly was going on with the equipment?"

"That, I don't know. The aid claims that her friend doesn't really go into detail, but a researcher goes to New Mexico Tech to investigate. I don't know what is discovered, but it's serious enough that a few people are dedicated solely to being in contact with the researchers at New Mexico Tech to share information."

Very interesting. I'm not sure what to think about all of this, but I have the feeling that this is something bigger than I had anticipated.

After sipping more on his drink, he continues, "Two days after the aid discloses this, Cody starts having crazy nightmares and the migraines and screaming start back up. Every day, it seems like it intensifies, and there are no answers. However, something unexpected starts to happen. Everyone that is involved with the research, including myself, starts to have nightmares. The nightmares aren't random. They all include Cody when he is younger in some type of onesie and a shadowy figure that takes the form of a huge black mass with red eyes or a person that's practically the outline of a human. The figure really doesn't say much, just three words: do not—"

"Interfere," I finish the line. The being's voice still haunts me when I'm awake.

"So you're having nightmares too, huh?" he asks with a surprised look.

"Yes. It only started recently, a couple of nights ago."

He slowly stands up and walks over to the window, gazing out in silence. He stands there for a while, and I can't help but wonder what's going through his mind.

"If you are getting the nightmares as well, this means that his power is growing. This is very frightening."

"Whose power? The boy's or this shadowy being?" I ask.

"Doctor, to be frank, I don't know, and that's the scary part about all of this. We can't understand how he's able to have this ability with dreams in the first place. Now we have some force that has amplified it and made it even worse. All the researchers in New

Mexico couldn't take it anymore, but we were pushed to keep going. This all changes, however, three weeks after Cody initially starts having these episodes. That morning starts off as usual, with all of us dreading to be at work due to the new developments. Then the team whose responsibility it is to be in coordination with New Mexico Tech comes rushing in and goes straight to the research managers' office. It's a closed-door meeting, but we can hear a little bit of what is being discussed. We don't know what they see at New Mexico Tech, but we do hear repeatedly the team telling the managers that they have to relocate the project immediately. It's my turn to make the coffee run that morning, so I leave before the meeting finishes. I'm a bit upset because I really want to know more information about why we need to relocate. I'm from New Mexico. It's my home and I love the fact that I'm able to be somewhat close to home while helping with this project. The thought of having to relocate frustrates me, and I have hopes that we will relocate to another part of the state."

His shoulders tense as he stares out the window, eyes narrowing while he scans the dimly lit street. The weight of his thoughts seems to press against the glass.

"Gary, it truly sounds like all of you endure a terrible and traumatic experience during those three weeks."

He turns around sharply. "I... I haven't even gotten to the worst part."

"Oh?"

"Yeah. It turns out I shouldn't have been frustrated that I had to go get coffee. Someone is definitely looking out for me that day," he responds with a serious tone.

My stomach begins to turn. I thought the nightmares they were having was the worst part of this whole thing.

"Gary, what happens? How does it end up being worse?" I ask.

"While I'm standing in line at the coffee shop, I receive a phone call from the aid that accidentally takes Cody to Datil. It takes me by surprise as she hardly calls me. I don't feel like answering the phone because I'm still frustrated that we may have to move, so I let it go to voicemail. I listen to the voicemail, and this is what she says."

He pulls out his phone and plays the voicemail.

"Whatever you do, DO NOT COME BACK! Do not come… Oh no, OH NO! Aaaaaah!"

"That's it. I immediately try to call back but it doesn't go through."

I'm in a state of shock. I don't know what to say, or think, or feel. I think a part of me is hoping that maybe she called while in a dream state and that maybe the dreams were too intense.

"Was she dreaming? Did she call you while she was in a dream?" I ask.

Gary continues to stare out the window. I can tell that whatever takes place, he is still traumatized from it. He lingers for five minutes, his expression unreadable. I can't tell if he is deep in thought about the question or too uneasy to respond.

He finally answers my question. "I don't know if she was or not. I rushed back to the facility, but the vicinity around it is blocked off. I park my car at a nearby business and decided to try and see if I can figure out what's going on at the facility. I'm able to get a decent vantage point a few blocks over. My stomach sinks at what I saw."

His eyes begin to well up, a few tears escape, and his whole demeanor shifts.

"Body bags everywhere. All of my colleagues are dead." He stops talking and then starts to weep uncontrollably.

Seeing Gary break down like that is jarring. From the moment we met, he has seemed so composed. He was careful with his words and seems to have been holding himself together. Now, it's like the dam has finally burst. I think he reached the breaking point today, recounting everything that happened. I go to him and attempt to console him. He stays like this for a good twenty minutes. He tries to get himself back together, but he is only partially successful.

"I left the area and went back home. I packed a decent amount of my clothes and essentials that I would need. I made the decision that I needed to leave Socorro immediately. I don't know where to go. I open up Maps, and I zoom out so the entire western United States fills the screen. I then decide to close my eyes, and wherever my finger touches is where I'll go. My finger ends up on Torrington, Wyoming. I have never been to Torrington, but it's far enough away from Socorro. I put on a baseball cap and sunglasses and withdraw from two ATMs in town. I don't want to leave a trail for anyone to find me. I get on the road, and I stop in Las Vegas, New Mexico, and go to a store to buy a memo pad, a hammer, and a phone. I used the memo pad to write down some numbers just in case I needed them. I activate the new phone and use the hammer to smash my personal and government phones. I then throw them away in a random dumpster and continued to make my way to Torrington."

Poor guy. He really has been through a lot, and I don't blame him for running. I'm sure investigators would've forced him to relive that trauma over and over again. There's no telling what they would've done to him, being the only one who survived. I then start to realize that the stakes in this are bigger than both of us. The thought of anyone dying because of this doesn't even cross my mind! I need to find answers. I need to know what exactly happens. If Secretary Jones won't give me the answers, then I will find them myself. The lives of others are at stake! I need to know how they ended up dead. I know I need to focus on Cody, but perhaps the key to what's happening with him can be found in their causes of death.

My mind then starts racing, going between thoughts and concerns. The one concern that really has me worried is the current researchers. I'm concerned for their safety… Oh no, they don't know what happened to the researchers in New Mexico! They were told that they would be briefed by them, but they are still waiting.

Should I tell them? The question is already weighing on me. Part of me wants to be honest, to lay everything out, but another part is hesitant, unsure of how much they really need to know right away. I think I'll hold off, at least until I learn more about what actually happens in Socorro. It's strange that Cody has not reacted this way the entire time he has been in Richmond, at least not until I get close. I will need to convince Dr. Hamilton to let me go to New Mexico to find answers.

I decide to ask Gary more questions, because with everything he has told me, I'm curious how he even knew to contact British Intelligence or me.

"How did you end up contacting me?"

"Well, Doctor, I would say you wouldn't believe me, but you did say you have the nightmares too, so you are aware that there's something bigger going on. Around the time your nightmares started, I start having dreams with Cody appearing in them. He hasn't been in my dreams since I left New Mexico, so this is a surprise. The mysterious figure isn't in the dreams, just a young Cody. He tells me to contact Director Lynne of British Intelligence to inform you of what has happened to me."

Everything seems to be communicated through dreams. I wonder why. I ask him, "Why did you listen to him? This seems like a big risk to take since you are trying to keep a low profile."

Gary starts staring at the ceiling. "It makes me nervous that he's able to communicate with me, even though I'm not in close proximity to Cody. Also, I did some research and found out that both you and Director Lynne are real people, so I knew that this was something I needed to do. Trust me, Dr. Koraline, I plan to head back to Wyoming as soon as I'm done here. I don't want to be near him more than I have to."

"You got here in a decent amount of time, coming from Wyoming."

"British Intelligence flew me here on a private charter flight with a Canadian company. They have been trying to get me to tell them what happened as well, but I don't trust them either," says Gary.

I'm glad to hear that he shares my concern about them.

"I don't trust them either, Gary, but they've been the only way I've been able to retrieve any information about what's taken place. I'm not sure how much of this I would share with them, to be honest," I say.

"I don't care what you tell them outside of one thing. DON'T TELL THEM ABOUT THE DEATH OF MY COLLEAGUES! They will deduce that I'm the only survivor and that will put me at risk."

"I understand, Gary. I will omit that when I give them information."

"Thank you."

It's clear he's ready for me to leave. We have finished our meal some time ago, and though he remains polite, there's a subtle shift in his demeanor over the past few minutes. His glances toward the alarm clock, the slight change in his tone; all suggest that our conversation has run its course.

"Well, Gary, I'm so sorry for your loss. I hope and pray that you'll find peace. Take care of yourself," I say.

"Thank you, Dr. Koraline. That really does mean so much to me."

I give him a hug and make my way back to my room. I have so much information to process. I do a quick look out of my window to make sure there is no suspicious activity nearby. I'm fearful that someone is going to discover that Gary is here. I don't see anything out of the ordinary, so I get out the laptop and contact Director Lynne.

I fill her in on everything except for the deaths.

Dir_Lynne: Is there any way that we can get in contact with his colleagues?

Dr_Kor: I'm afraid not. He has not seen them since he went into hiding.

Dir_Lynne: I see. Why did he go into hiding again?

Dr_Kor: The nightmares were getting to him, he couldn't take it anymore.

I have to lie about why he leaves because I realize that the phone call from that aid would be a red flag, and Director Lynne would think that they are dead.

Dir_Lynne: That's unfortunate. It would be nice to get some more pieces to this complicated puzzle. There's some information I can pass on to you. We didn't really consider this too important until you told us about the VLA and New Mexico Tech.

Dr_Kor: Oh? What's the intel?

Dir_Lynne: A couple of days before Washington contacted you, the US-based National Science Foundation sent a request to radio telescopes in the UK, Russia, Chile, Australia, and Japan to focus in on a certain quadrant of space. Details aren't given on what they were listening for.

Dr_Kor: Huh. Weird. I'll see if I can find out anything else.

Dir_Lynne: Thanks. Keep us posted. Goodnight.

Chat ends.

Something happened at the VLA in New Mexico, and I'm determined to find out what. But first, I'm going to get some rest. This is against my better judgment, but I really need it. My body is drained, and the moment I lie down on the bed, I fall asleep.

Chapter 9

Unlocking the Secrets

The Fourth Dream

I find myself on a beach. It feels very calm and relaxing. I'm glad to be in a normal environment. However, I know something has to be weird. Every place I've been to with Cody in my dreams has been very strange or connected to him in some way. So, I start to walk along the beach, and I notice something interesting: I can only hear the waves crashing. I see birds flying overhead, but I can't hear them. I can't hear my feet pressing into the sand either.

"This place is peaceful but weird," I say to myself.

I know it won't be long until I run into Cody. I also keep my eye out for that mysterious being. I know he'll be making an appearance too. I look around me and feel puzzled because I've never been to a beach like this. To the right of me is the ocean as far as the eye can see, and to the left of me is the beach. It's not the kind of beach surrounded by boardwalks or beachfront homes. There are no hotels lining the shore, no lifeguard towers, and no signs of civilization in sight. It's isolated. Just open sand, though the sand seems to go on forever, and crashing waves. This location appears to be entirely undisturbed. I'm not sure what to think, but I figure I need to continue walking.

Though unique, it's pleasant to feel the sand and waves at my feet from time to time. It's satisfying, relaxing. I'm really enjoying myself. However, I know I can't let my guard down.

I continue to walk for ten minutes, and then I think I hear a noise coming from the ocean. I stop and examine the water to see if anything looks out of the ordinary. After not seeing anything, I decide to keep walking. But when I look out in front of me, I see something in the distance. I can't tell what it is, but I know it's not a person. I pick up the pace so I can get to the object quicker. The closer it comes into view, the more puzzled I am.

"Is that a box?"

I'm not quite sure if it's a box or something that just resembles one. I get within about twenty feet of it and see what it is. It's a chest. What is a chest doing out here in the middle of the beach? What is the meaning of this chest? I try to open it, but it's locked. I look closer and am surprised to see that the chest has four keyholes. Above each keyhole is a different symbol. The first keyhole has an owl above it, the second a lion, the third a horse, and the fourth a pocket watch.

Huh. I wonder if the key I received in the last dream will work with one of these keyholes. I check to see if the key is still in my pocket and to my surprise, it is! Well, if I'm being honest, nothing surprises me at this point.

With everything that has been going on, I realize I haven't taken the time to properly look at the key since I first received it. It's an antique-style key, detailed with an owl perched at the top of the handle and a circle framing it. I decide to go to the first keyhole to insert the key, but then out of nowhere, the ground begins to shake violently. I fall back on the chest and it sinks into the sand. I'm not sure what the source of the shaking is, but I have a feeling.

The shaking stops, and I try to move the sand to find the chest. I don't have any luck and I start to despair. Fortunately, I still have the key in my hand, and I fear that the mysterious being is going to try to come after it. As much as I want to find the chest again, I know that keeping the key away from that being is my top priority. Even if I don't fully understand why. So, I begin to run. I'm on the move for a good bit. I do have a sharp realization of how hard it is to run on the sand.

I come to a stop, doubled over and gasping for breath. As I try to recover, I suddenly feel a hand on my shoulder. The unexpected touch frightens me, and I lose my balance, collapsing to the ground. When I look up, I see Cody standing there. However, there's something about him that's different. It's definitely him, but he looks slightly older, like time has passed since I last saw him in the previous dreams. Maybe two years older, judging by his face and posture. Without saying a word, he reaches out his hand and helps me to my feet.

He then starts to speak, "The chest is nearby. I had to move it because I sensed his presence."

"The mysterious being that keeps showing up in these dreams?"

"Yes. Him." Cody's demeanor shifts from confidence to total fear. I figure this is my chance to ask him more questions about this being.

"Cody, the mysterious being, who is he?"

"I don't know. He's been in my dreams ever since Lauren took me to Datil," he responds.

"Datil? Oh yeah, the town, the aid; I take it her name was Lauren, who took you there on accident?"

Cody gives me a searching look but then starts looking at the ground again and answers me. "Yes. You're correct."

"I noticed your face and body language when I brought that up. I take it there's more to the story than what I've been told already. Am I right?"

Cody slowly looks up at me, but before he can answer, the ground shakes again. This time, it feels more violent than the previous occurrence. In the midst of the shaking, I see the chest about a hundred yards from me.

"I found the chest!"

However, when I look over to where Cody was standing, he's gone. I don't have time to find out where he went. Using all my strength, I walk to the chest as everything shakes around me. It seems like the shaking becomes more violent the closer I get to the chest. I fall to the ground a couple of times, but I'm able to get back up and keep going. I do eventually get to the chest and the shaking stops abruptly. With the key in hand, I place it in the first keyhole and turn it. I start to hear what sounds like mechanical noises coming from inside the chest. As soon as the sounds from the chest stop, a very bright light blinds me. Thirty seconds pass and the light slowly dims. I find myself sitting in the back of a car.

I don't recognize the car, nor do I recognize the driver, but I do recognize Cody sitting in the passenger seat. I look out my window, but I don't recognize where we are. The topography, however, is familiar to me, and I deduce that we are out west somewhere. My assumption is New Mexico as I come to the conclusion that I'm in one of Cody's memories. The aid, Lauren, begins to talk to Cody.

"Cody, there's a lot going on that you don't understand. I know you're wondering where we're going, but you'll be okay. I just have to take care of something."

Cody looks at her with a frustrated look. "What do you have to take care of? There is nothing out here."

"I have a boss outside of the facility that I have to contact," Lauren responds. "My supervisors at the facility wouldn't understand, so I have to do this far away from them."

"Who is this boss that you have to secretly contact?" asks Cody.

"Well, Cody, he's the… and he's very powerful and very dangerous."

The conversation pauses briefly. After a short silence, Cody speaks.

"If he's so powerful and dangerous, why did you bring me out here to contact him? Couldn't you have done it after you dropped me off at the facility?" Cody inquires, his tone clearly reflecting his concern.

"My boss is interested in you. I thought it'd be useful to have you close."

This revelation unsettles me, but it explains why she drives past Magdalena. I've traveled out west numerous times. Towns are few and far apart. Although it's easy to miss a small town, I find it hard to believe she accidentally drove past Magdalena. I'm not sure why, but I have a gut feeling that we're not getting the whole story. I have questions about her boss.

Cody looks at Lauren very sternly and asks, "Why is he interested in me? Is it because of my dreams?"

"Yes, Cody. It's because of your dreams. You have a gift that my boss is interested in."

They continue to talk, but I'm not sure what's happening because I can't hear them anymore. I try to read their lips, but I'm unsuccessful for the most part.

Not too long after I lose the ability to hear them, the car comes to a stop. I look out the window to my left and see a field full of satellites. This must be the VLA Gary was referring to. I don't get it. Why stop here? We don't stop for long. We get back on the road until we reach Datil. Lauren stops at a small store and gets out of the car.

I'm torn on what to do. I want to stay in the car and see if it's true about Cody's migraine starting. But I also want to see if Lauren is contacting her boss outside of the car. I make the decision to get out of the car, but I quickly find out that the door is locked. I try to unlock it, but I notice there's no mechanism to lock or unlock it from the inside. I look at the driver's side door panel but see that there's no mechanism nor a button to unlock the doors there either. Seeing that my plan is thwarted, I decide to observe Cody. Nothing happens. Cody just looks outside every once in a while, and then plays on his phone. Lauren is gone for ten minutes. I assume she makes contact with her boss and makes some purchases. She comes out of the store with a bag, and I can tell that there are drinks and a few snacks.

What is she up to? Is she going to give Cody away to her boss? That's the only explanation on my mind for why she brought him out here. Huh! I wonder if her boss works at the VLA. Maybe another set of researchers is planning to pay her a decent amount of money to bring Cody to them? Whatever is planned doesn't succeed, as Cody remains present. I simply observe to understand the situation. We start making our way back to Socorro. Cody grabs a soda and a snack and continues to mind his own business.

After driving for a bit, I notice we start to slow down again. I look out the right window and see that we're stopping in front of the VLA again. She may have called him from the store to say she had Cody. I expect to see someone standing outside or for Lauren to get on the phone. She does get out of the car, but she just stands there. She doesn't get on her phone, and her body language doesn't indicate she's looking for somebody. She just stands still, facing the VLA facility.

After ten minutes, Cody knocks on her window and asks what she's doing. Lauren ignores him and keeps standing there. Five more minutes pass, and suddenly I see Cody rubbing his forehead intensely. I wonder if his migraine has started. I start to see a few tears on his cheek. Cody then begins to cry intensely, and the crying soon escalates to screaming.

As soon as he starts screaming, Lauren gets back into the car and we start to drive off. Lauren looks unfazed by the screaming. She turns to him, places her hand on his shoulder, and says, "Don't be afraid, Cody. Your time has come."

The bright light appears again. I can't see anything. As the light dims, I find myself back on that strange beach. The mysterious figure stands in front of me. He's in the same form he had in the last dream, the one inside my old office: a humanlike shape with red eyes and a black trench coat. His entire body and the coat seem made of the same solid darkness. He's staring at me with those red eyes. Spine-chilling.

He begins to speak in his creepy, terrifying voice, "You shouldn't have seen that. He's trying to fight back. He won't win. We are tired of everyone interfering, especially you. We'll do what we must to bring order again. I'll start by getting rid of you."

My stomach sinks. I slowly back away, but he starts coming toward me at a fast pace. I know I can't escape, but I can at least try to run. So, I turn and take off in the opposite direction. He's not far behind, and I feel like I'm not running fast enough. Right when he's about to catch me, the beach in front of me collapses, and there's nothing but black underneath me. I start to fall, screaming uncontrollably. As I fall, I look up toward the place where my descent began and see the being standing there. His voice reaches me with the closeness of someone speaking just beside me:

"YOU CANNOT STOP ME."

Then, huge red eyes pierce the blackness, and a massive hand comes out and tries to grab me.

I wake up.

I'm in a cold sweat, my chest tightening as I struggle to breathe. I start hyperventilating so much I feel like I'm suffocating. My heart pounds against my ribs, and the dizziness grows worse with every second. I try to stand and make it to the bathroom, thinking cold water might help, but my legs give out beneath me. I hit the floor hard, but barely feel it. Everything is spinning and I can't make it stop.

What's happening to me? A panic attack? A heart issue? I don't know. Whatever this is, I'm spiraling, and I'm losing control.

I croak out a plea to my phone and tell the virtual assistant to call 911.

"9-1-1, what's your emergency?"

"Help! I…need…help! I…feel…" My words come in broken gasps.

"Are you experiencing a medical emergency?"

"I…am…I'll be out…side…my ho…tel…room," I say, barely.

The phone slips a little in my hand as I start crawling, dragging myself toward the door. The operator's voice crackles softly from the speaker, growing more urgent with each unanswered question.

"Ma'am, can you hear me? Are you still there?"

I reach the door with trembling fingers and struggle to lift the phone. I can barely hold it, but I press it against my ear just enough to hear. The operator's voice is clearer, closer, so real.

"Stay with me. Are you able to speak?"

With the last of my strength, I crack the door open and whisper, "I'm… out… side. Help me, ple…"

Before I finish speaking, everything fades.

Chapter 10

Revelations

When I open my eyes, I find myself in a hospital bed. I feel weak and stiff. I start looking around the room slowly and find my assistant Melanie sitting to the right of me. She is busy on her phone but soon realizes that I'm awake.

"Dr. Koraline! You're awake! How do you feel?"

I try to talk, but my mouth is too dry. I signal to her for a drink and she brings me water. As I start taking sips, I notice an IV is hooked up to me and I have to be careful not to pull it out. I'm finally able to talk.

"I feel weak. I'm not sure what happened. I started feeling dizzy and the next thing I knew, I blacked out."

"Lucky for you, the person in the room next to you heard you collapse and called 9-1-1. They gave the dispatcher the information needed, like your room number. You passed out before you could finish the call. You have a mild concussion, but other than that, everything's good. They are attributing stress as to why you possibly passed out. They wanted to speak with you when you woke up. However, I'll wait a little bit before telling the nurses so you have some time to process things," says Melanie.

"Thank you, Melanie. I appreciate having some time to adjust before they return. May I ask how you found out I was at the hospital?"

"I came by this morning to pick you up. I tried to call you multiple times, but your phone kept going to voicemail. I also knocked several times and that's when your neighbor informed me that you were at the hospital."

I'm glad Melanie is here. However, I realize Melanie will want to know what stressed me out, so I try to decide how to explain. After about fifteen minutes of silence, she finally speaks.

"What do you think caused you to pass out?"

I'm not sure how much I should tell Melanie. After the dream I had before ending up here, my trust in others is uncertain, especially considering it was an assistant who may have harmed Cody in New Mexico if that dream is true. Still, I need all the help I can get to figure out what is going on. So, I decide to tell her about the dream.

"I had a very intense dream last night. It was Cody."

Melanie starts to look nervous, but she presses on, "Oh? What happened?"

"It was…" I stop myself. I have to be very careful how I word this. Even though I'm willing to take a risk on her, I don't want to reveal that I have information from a foreign nation and Gary. I limit my comments to only what I have recently dreamed.

"It was a strange dream. I remember being on a beach and seeing Cody before some shadowy figure starts chasing me. I fall into an abyss, and suddenly I'm in the back of a car with Cody and a woman I don't recognize. She mentions something about her boss wanting to meet him. We stop twice at the VLA, and at one point, Cody starts breaking down, sobbing and rubbing his head. The woman doesn't seem to care; she just keeps driving like nothing is wrong. That's all I can remember."

I choose not to share any more information for now. If I feel more comfortable opening up to her or her colleagues later on, I'll say that I remember more details about the dream afterward.

Melanie looks perplexed; she isn't sure how to take the information I give her.

She eventually responds, "What is the VLA? Do you think it's possible that this dream is an indication of what went on in New Mexico? I hope it is. It's insane that we still haven't been given any information about why Cody was moved here."

I feel bad about withholding information from her. I can only imagine how overwhelming it must be for this team, being left in the dark about everything that has been happening. It's messed up that I found out more about Cody in the past thirty-six hours than they have in months.

"The VLA is a place out in New Mexico that has multiple radios that look like huge satellite dishes that listen for radio signals from space. Yes, Melanie, I do believe the dream may be an indication of what occurred in New Mexico."

"What does the VLA have to do with this?" Melanie asks.

"I don't know. I'm hoping that we can find some answers real soon. Anyways, does anyone else know that I'm in the hospital?"

"Yes," Melanie responds. "Dr. Hamilton instructed me to stay here until they discharge you."

"Am I expected to come to the facility after I'm discharged?"

"Unfortunately, yes. Dr. Hamilton wants to get to the bottom of this as quickly as possible," responds Melanie.

"I understand. I'm okay with that anyway. I don't want to be cooped up in a hotel room all day."

A nurse comes in and sees that I'm awake. "Dr. Koraline, we're happy to see you awake. I'm going to ask you a few questions concerning you passing out. Have you been under a lot of stress lately?"

Talk about an understatement!

"Yes, I have, it's been a very stressful couple of days coming here from the UK."

The nurse continues with his questions, "Do you think the traveling is the main source of your stress? If you don't mind me asking, why have you traveled here?"

I'm not quite sure what to say. I know I can't even give a hint as to what I'm doing. So, I come up with an answer on the fly.

"I'm here to work on a big project. I've been extremely stressed about this project for months now, and it was overwhelming when I got here in person to help out."

I think that's a good answer.

The nurse goes on, "This must be an important project if it has you this stressed. The doctor thinks it might be stress-related, since all your test results came back normal. Do you have any existing health conditions we should know about?"

"No, I don't," I reply.

"Okay then, Doctor, you're free to go. I'll bring your discharge papers and afterward, you can head on out."

He steps out and is back in less than five minutes. I'm shocked by how quickly he returns with the discharge paperwork. I decide to look at the paperwork as he unhooks me from the IV.

"Have a good rest of your day, Doctor. Your aftercare instructions are in the paperwork."

"Thank you," I say to him as I continue looking at the paperwork. The first thing I notice really takes me by surprise.

The discharge date and time:

Sunday, July 16, 2023. 4:15 p.m.

I wait for the nurse to finish unhooking me and placing a Band-Aid over where the IV had been before talking to Melanie. He leaves the room.

I quickly look over to Melanie. "Have I really been unconscious for that long?"

I don't have my phone on me, so I haven't had the chance to check the time. I'm not sure where the clock is in this room. I need confirmation that this is in fact the time.

"Yeah, you were out of it for hours."

I was thinking it's late morning or early afternoon, not almost evening!

"You still might be a little weak, so I'll push you in a wheelchair and then I'll pick you up from the exit," Melanie suggests.

"Thanks, Melanie."

Melanie goes to find a wheelchair as I slowly get dressed. She comes in with the wheelchair and I slowly get in. She's right; I'm still feeling weak. Maybe some food will help. We get to the entrance and she goes to get her car. While she's retrieving the car, I hear a faint, weird voice. I don't recognize it at first. I have no clue where the voice is coming from; I don't see anyone. Maybe it's in my head?

"YOU'VE INTERFERED TOO MUCH."

The voice cuts through like a blade, clear, and unmistakable. I freeze. I know that voice. It's not just in my head, and it's not part of a dream. He's speaking to me while I'm awake. The mysterious being has crossed into my waking world. Panic rises in my chest. I hate when he speaks to me in dreams, but at least then, I can take comfort in knowing it all vanishes when I open my eyes. Now, that comfort is gone. He took it from me. I'm not sure what my next steps are, but I know I need energy to confront whatever is next.

Melanie pulls up in the car and she assists me in getting in.

"Hey Melanie, can we get something to eat before we get to the facility?"

"Umm, sure. You'll have to eat it on the way. Dr. Hamilton is expecting you."

We leave and head to a fast-food restaurant. When we pull around to pay, I realize Melanie is going to pay for me, and I feel a bit guilty for asking to stop for food. Once I get my meal and drink, I start eating as quickly as I can, given the state I'm in. The food helps me tremendously. I'm still not at 100 percent, but I feel way better than I did before. While we are on our way, I start to contemplate my options. I don't want to tell Melanie, Dr. Hamilton, and the others about the information I've received. I don't know if I can fully trust them or not.

However, it does cross my mind that I may have a moral obligation to tell them after learning about the team in New Mexico. So, I decide that I'll ask some questions and use my best judgment to determine whether to let them in on everything I know. I don't know if I should tell them the sources of this information or be as vague as possible. I do, however, consider that they may not believe me if I don't give up my sources. All I know is that I need a team that will not only support me but also understands what is really happening.

I'm also curious how Cody is going to react this time. Is my presence going to upset him again? More importantly, if Lauren, the aid in New Mexico, somehow set off Cody by attempting to contact her boss, how did I set him off? I have no connection to Lauren or her boss in any way.

When we arrive, Melanie guides me to a different entrance than the one we used before. As we approach the door, a wave of panic hits me; I don't have my badge! But before I can say anything, Melanie hands it to me. She grabbed it ahead of time from my belongings at the hospital, and with that small relief, we continue inside. As we enter through the door, I see that it leads into a big office. Dr. Hamilton is sitting at his desk at the far end.

"Dr. Koraline! I'm glad to see you! How are you feeling? Are you okay?"

"Yes. I'm doing much better," I respond.

"I want to apologize to you for bringing you over here right after getting out of the hospital. Unfortunately, we've had some new developments that are adding to this mystery even more."

"Oh? What's going on?" I ask as I walk over to one of his chairs and take a seat. Melanie sits in the chair next to me.

"Cody started screaming again not long after you left. Worse than he did when you came by yesterday. The strange thing is when he started screaming this time, the staff that was in the room with him started to have intense migraines and couldn't continue to work. I thought maybe the screaming was getting to them, but the weird thing is the migraines stopped as soon as they left the room. I thought this was an excuse for them not to be in the room when he was screaming, but when I walked into the room, I also experienced an intense migraine. It brought me to tears, that's how bad it was. I don't cry easily. I ended up leaving the room and just like the rest of the staff, my migraine disappeared instantly," Dr. Hamilton recalls.

I start fearing the worst. Is this team about to meet the same fate as the team in New Mexico?

He continues to speak. "It gets even weirder. After I left here and went home and went to bed, I found myself in a weird dream. I found myself in the middle of a dark forest and above the tree line was a shadowy, mysterious being with red eyes. Cody was off in the distance. The mysterious being looked straight at me and said, YOU'VE INTERFERED ENOUGH! Cody then disappeared and I woke up from the dream in a cold sweat."

Dr. Hamilton looks out of it. I notice that he is subtly shaking.

"Were you the only one to have a dream?" I ask.

"No, everyone else that went into that room had dreams, too. They all dreamed the exact same thing I did. Doctor, I know you know as much as I do, but what's going on? This is unlike anything I've ever experienced. There's no logical explanation for what took place. I'm on the verge of calling up Washington and demanding answers before I quit! I'm at the point that I don't care what the consequences are for giving up!"

I don't know if it's because I'm feeling sympathy for him and the team or not, but something in my gut tells me that I need to tell them everything I know. I take a deep breath and start to talk.

"Dr. Hamilton, I'm about to tell you some information. I originally wasn't going to tell you because of how I came about this information, but I now think it's imperative for everyone here to know. I obtained most of this information in the past twenty-four hours," I say to him.

Dr. Hamilton sits back in his chair in disbelief. "So, you were planning to hide information from me like they are doing in Washington?"

"Not exactly," I reply. "I was going to reveal what I needed to, but the information that I recently discovered is very alarming."

Dr. Hamilton still looks unsure, but he doesn't have a choice. "Okay, Dr. Koraline, what do you have to tell us?"

"Before I go any further, I should explain how I came across this information and what was asked of me. Right after Secretary Jones contacted me, the Director of MI6 reached out to me. She expressed concerns with this project. However, their intelligence believed that the US government was working on a way to turn dreams into reality. She gave me a laptop to communicate with her. I only told her what I thought she needed to know because I didn't trust her like I don't trust the US government. She did, however, give me information that gave me a few pieces of the puzzle. She eventually connected me with a man known only as Gary. He unveiled some very crucial information. This guy didn't work for the British. He used to work on this project in New Mexico," I say, my nerves on edge as I wait for his response.

"You got in touch with someone who worked on this in New Mexico? We've been awaiting reports about what went down in Socorro!" Dr. Hamilton exclaims. He has the look of a desperate man in his eyes.

"Yes, I did. However, you have to understand, I only found out about him yesterday after I had left here. So, I really didn't hide anything from you, if that's what you're thinking. No, I didn't say anything to Melanie because I really wanted to get a sense from more than one person who worked here if I could trust all of you. No offense, Melanie."

"None taken. We don't know each other and everything about this project has been shrouded in mystery so I don't blame you," says Melanie.

I was so glad that Melanie understood.

I continue where I left off. "According to Gary, the team in New Mexico had no issues with Cody at first. They were confused by his dream-related behavior, but nothing alarming happened. That changed when an aid named Lauren took him on an unauthorized trip. She was supposed to pick up a misdelivered package in Magdalena but claimed she got lost because of poor GPS signal. While passing the VLA near Datil, Cody suddenly became unhinged. His behavior worsened over the following weeks. One day, while Gary was out getting coffee, Lauren called him in a panic. When he returned, the facility was blocked off, and he later learned that everyone inside had died. Terrified by what happened, Gary went into hiding and worked to keep his identity secret."

Dr. Hamilton and Melanie look like they were both trying to process everything. I cannot blame them. I have known this information longer than they have, and I'm still trying to wrap my head around it. I notice that Dr. Hamilton was looking off in the space with a blank stare.

"Dr. Koraline, I'm not even sure where to start. I have so many questions I want to ask," says Dr. Hamilton.

"While you're sorting through your questions, Doctor, I have one I want to ask you, Dr. Koraline. If Gary went into hiding, how did he get in touch with you?" Melanie asks.

"He had a dream. I know I shouldn't just take someone at their word simply because they claim to have received instructions in a dream. But when Cody shows up in both of our most recent dreams, completely unprompted, it's hard not to believe there's something more to it. Especially since he had no way of knowing that Cody had been appearing in mine."

The three of us sit in silence for a while. I wasn't sure what was next. I did expect more questions at least. Dr. Hamilton did look like he was in deep thought. After a while, he gets out his phone and I hear that he's texting someone.

Then, Dr. Hamilton spoke, "Dr. Koraline, may I have you sit in our lobby area? The team and I have some things we need to discuss. Thank you for sharing this information with us, I will let you know when you can come back into the office."

I get up and gently say, "You're welcome," before I slowly make my way to the lobby.

When I get to the lobby, five people come out of the other door and head towards Dr. Hamilton's office. They don't even acknowledge that I was there. I wasn't sure what's being discussed, but it's taking a while. I remain seated in the lobby, unsure of what I was supposed to do. The stillness around me only made the waiting worse. Should I stay here? I keep glancing around, hoping for some kind of sign or direction, but nothing. Then, a thought comes to my head.

I'm going to talk to Cody.

No one told me I couldn't. I was just instructed to wait out here. Dr. Hamilton probably won't be thrilled about this, but right now, I feel like I have the strongest connection to Cody. Besides, I was brought here to help in some way, and that's exactly what I intend to do. The security guard is minding his own business when I walk up to him. I take out my badge as I approach.

"You're going in there? Good luck."

That does not exactly inspire confidence. He presses a button, and a loud noise comes from the door. I expect him to tell me I cannot go in, but he says nothing. It feels like he has been waiting for me to make my way back here. I open the door and step through, heading into the room on the right where he was earlier. He's not there. I glance down the hallway and see four more rooms: two on the right, including the one I just checked, and two on the left. The hallway stretches at least two hundred feet, which surprises me since I never realized how much space is back here. I begin walking slowly down the hall, unsure of which room Cody is in. Every door except the first one is closed. I don't know if they are locked, but even so, I plan to try each one.

As I approach the first door, I hear a whisper out of nowhere. "Don't come any closer."

I stop in my tracks, startled. It sounds like Cody, but I keep moving forward, slowly and cautiously.

The whisper grows louder. "Listen…do not come any closer."

I stop again. Am I making a wise decision here? Should I listen to this voice and return to the lobby? I stand there, thinking for a moment. No, I'm not going to listen. I need to find out more about what's happening. I push past the fear and move forward. I reach the first door on the left and try the handle. It's locked.

As I continue down the hall, the whisper grows louder until it reaches a normal speaking volume, "Has anyone told you before that you're stubborn?"

The voice slithers through the air, I don't respond. I just keep moving, my steps quickening. A strange purple glow pulses softly beneath the last door on the right. It's flickering like a heartbeat, silent yet persistent, as if something otherworldly is stirring behind the door. Something is in there. My pulse jumps. That has to be where Cody is. I go for the doorknob.

"LEAVE! NOW! DO NOT INTERFERE!"

I freeze. I now really start to question my choices. Should I proceed? Should I leave? I then start to replay the voice in my head. It doesn't sound like Cody, or at least completely like Cody. His voice had merged with that of the mysterious being. What if I'm here to save Cody and this being is trying to stop me? I take a deep breath, and I attempt to open the door. It is unlocked. As I look into the room, I realize that I made a grave mistake.

Chapter 11

The Encounter

The room is filled with a black and purple veil, and all I can hear are screams. I don't recognize the screams, but the atmosphere is terrifying. Cody is standing in the middle of the room, surrounded by the veil; his eyes are closed. I'm terrified, yet I keep moving closer to him. With each step, the room around me seems to fade, consumed by the presence of the veil. It gives off a deep, pulsing violet light that shimmers like heat waves rising from pavement. The closer I get, the more overpowering it becomes. It's thick, electric, almost alive. It wraps around everything, casting shadows that don't belong and humming with a quiet energy that makes my skin tingle.

The room no longer feels like a room at all. It's as if I have stepped into the veil itself. I also notice that the closer I get to him, the more the screams begin to fade. I keep going until I'm standing about five feet in front of him. I can't see any of the room and this mysterious veil is everywhere. He opens his eyes, and to my surprise, they are red. His eyes remind me of the mysterious being's eyes. My guess is the being has taken over Cody's body. I want to communicate with him, and I need to gain as much information as possible. I'm not sure how he will respond to me, but I go ahead and take the first step.

"Who are you?"

"I have numerous names, but you can call me Salus."

Salus… that's a weird name. I make a mental note of it so I can research later.

"As far as gaining more information, it's not time for you to have the full picture. That'll come in due time." I notice that I can no longer hear Cody's voice; I can only hear Salus's.

"Why don't you just tell me now?" I say, frustrated, not knowing whether I'm making a mistake.

"As I've mentioned, it's not time for you to have the full picture."

This isn't helping; I just want answers and don't understand why he won't tell me. Unless whatever he's planning is not fully ready yet. I begin to hear a low growl, and he's visibly growing angry. Tension moves through his posture like a storm ready to break. I don't understand why he is reacting this way. I haven't even said anything to him.

Wait… I just realized he mentioned something about me gaining more information. I never said that out loud, I only thought it… No way.

He is reading my thoughts.

"How perceptive. You're smarter than I gave you credit for," he says with an evil smile.

What do I do? I'm not sure. If he can read my thoughts, then I need to leave this room as soon as possible! I begin slowly walking backward, but that evil smile quickly disappears.

"Where do you think you're going?" he says in a low growl with his fists clenched at his sides.

I'm not sure what he's going to do next. Then, I'm saved by the most unexpected thing; an alarm. The piercing sound causes Salus to screech. Cody's body collapses to the floor. The mysterious black and purple veil disappears. Dr. Hamilton and the others come rushing into the room.

"Dr. Koraline! What are you doing in here? Have you been in here the whole time?"

"Yes, Dr. Hamilton, I have been in here," I reply.

He looks horrified by my response. "How long have you been back here?"

"I can't give you precise timing. However, I got tired of waiting in the lobby and I want to see Cody again. I want to talk to him, but Salus appeared." As I speak, I can see Dr. Hamilton's face turn from concern to frustration.

"Dr. Koraline, who is Salus?" He tilts his head and squints at me.

"It's the same mysterious being that has appeared in the dreams. When I entered the room, a black and purple veil surrounded it, and Cody's voice sounds like a blend of his and Salus's at first. I hear screams, but as I get closer, only his voice remains and the veil thickens. Salus refuses to share anything beyond his name, saying it is not my time to know more. I don't know why he holds back, but I quickly realize he can read my thoughts. He grew angry when he sensed I was trying to run. I was thinking that something was going to happen to me, but then the alarm goes off. Why did it go off?"

"It goes off because the black and purple veil showed up on our camera and we couldn't see what was going on in the room," replies Melanie. "We have never seen this happen before and we were worried about Cody. So, we sounded the alarm we have in case something happens with Cody."

"I see. Does it really take the camera that long to recognize something is wrong?" I ask, wondering why no one came sooner.

"We review the ten-second loop before the alarm goes off. The only thing it shows is Cody standing in the middle of the room. Then the veil shows up out of nowhere. That's why we were surprised that you were back here," says Dr. Hamilton.

Wow. So, the alarm really did possibly save my life. I'm getting more concerned with how much control Cody, or Salus, I don't know which one, is gaining in the real world. Dreams are one thing, but things are being impacted in reality.

"Are you upset with me that I'm back here?" I ask.

"I'm not, Dr. Koraline, but next time, let at least one of the other staffers know. We try not to be around him by ourselves. It's not that we suspect our staff of doing anything, more so the fact that we have practically zero prior information about Cody."

"I understand."

We continue to talk and discuss various possibilities for what it means that Salus is making appearances outside of dreams. We shift our attention to what comes next.

"What's the next step?" asks Melanie.

Dr. Hamilton looks deep in thought. I wonder if he is considering Salus and what I told him about the incident in New Mexico. I know he wants to learn more about Cody, but the safety of his staff must be weighing heavily on him.

"To be frank, I don't know, Melanie. I think our first priority is to come up with a safety plan in case things go haywire." He stops, trying to think of words to say. "Just to be safe, you know."

Dr. Hamilton seems to be choosing his words carefully. I have a feeling he doesn't share what I tell him with the rest of the staff, which is probably for the best. I can only imagine the panic it would cause if everyone knew what had happened.

"Okay, everyone, back to work. Dr. Koraline, Melanie, follow me."

Melanie and I follow Dr. Hamilton outside the facility into the parking lot. He looks back to see if anyone followed us.

"Dr. Koraline, here's what we need to do. I would love nothing more than for Cody to be out of this facility, but I know that's not possible right now. We do, however, need answers and we need them fast. So, here's what I suggest we do. The two of you should go to Socorro to find answers. I can't think of a good cover story to use to get the two of you out there, but at this point, I don't care because our lives are on the line."

I understand where he's coming from, but maybe a phone call will suffice.

"I have a better idea. Why don't we contact New Mexico Tech and ask them what they are collaborating with the researchers about? Gary tells me that after Cody is near the VLA, a select few of the staff remain in constant contact with the researchers at New Mexico Tech who use the VLA."

"That would be easier to do. However, I'm concerned that they may be hesitant or not able to give us the information. I know that's a risk if you go in person, but I feel like we'd have more luck," says Dr. Hamilton.

"Good point." I accept that Dr. Hamilton is probably right, but then I think of a possible way we might still be able to get the information.

"What if we call them, explain what we're working on, and tell them the current status of the staff they were in contact with who worked on the project? It's risky, but if we have no idea what happened to those people, there's a good chance they don't know either. We might be able to use that to pressure them into giving us the information," I suggest.

"You're right, that's very risky. It may work, but if they contact anyone about what has taken place, then Washington will know that we are poking around," says Dr. Hamilton.

"Don't we run that risk going there in person as well?" says Melanie.

"How about this? Why don't you and Melanie get a burner phone and contact New Mexico Tech? See what answers you can get. If they are hesitant to give you information, then we will go with my plan and the two of you go there in person. Does that sound good?" Dr. Hamilton suggests.

I don't respond immediately. I think through the pros and cons. My plan is more convenient, but they might not give us much since they can't verify who we are. Dr. Hamilton's plan gives us more legitimacy, but traveling there could be dangerous if Salus can appear in the real world. There is no guarantee we will make it back. Either way, we need answers.

"Okay, Dr. Hamilton, let's go with your idea. We will attempt contact via phone and we'll make the trip out there if the phone call produces little to no results."

Dr. Hamilton nods in acknowledgment.

"Melanie, do you agree with Dr. Hamilton?"

I want to ensure that I include Melanie, especially since she looks like she's not 100% on board.

"I agree with Dr. Hamilton, but if we're going to do this, we need to take serious precautions," Melanie says. "I'm almost certain our phones are being tracked. That means we, along with the rest of the staff, can't keep carrying them around like nothing's changed. If Washington gets even the slightest idea of what we're planning, their response will be severe. Since they never shared this information with us to begin with, there's no reason to think they'll handle this fairly. We need to ditch our phones and make sure we leave no trail behind," says Melanie.

"You're right. I do believe they would take extreme measures. However, the threat posed by Cody and Salus is far greater than Washington. We need to know what we are dealing with here," says Dr. Hamilton.

"I do have my concerns, as we all do, but Cody and Salus concern me more," says Melanie.

"Ladies, good luck. To minimize the possibility of Washington knowing, wait until you see me in person to give me any information."

"Sounds good. Please be careful. This Salus being is dangerous and we should exercise extreme caution," I say sternly.

Dr. Hamilton makes his way back to the building and Melanie and I jump in her car.

"Should we go to a drugstore or a Dollar General store to get a burner?" I ask Melanie.

"We could, but there is a truck stop not far from us that we could go to get one."

"Let's go," Melanie responds.

We head to the truck stop and buy a cheap smartphone since there are no flip phones available. We talk very little in the car. I think we're both nervous about what we are doing. We decide that we will make the phone call at my hotel room to have as much privacy as possible. Melanie finds the number to New Mexico Tech and I have her call. I would make the call, but Melanie has been assigned to this project longer than I have, so I figure she will sound more official.

"Are you ready?"

"I'm as ready as I'm going to be, Doctor."

She dials the number and puts it on speaker. We get the automated system.

This is the New Mexico Institute of Mining and Technology. Please listen to the following options.

"Melanie, with all of the craziness that's going on, I just realized something."

"What's up?" Melanie looks frustrated as she tries to listen to the prompts.

"It's Sunday. There's probably no one there."

"It is Sunday, isn't it? Maybe we can at least leave a message."

We wait impatiently through the prompts until we reach the physics department. We don't know which department the VLA belongs to, but we figure this is our best guess. The phone rings for a good bit. We both expect to reach the voicemail box. However, much to our surprise, someone picks up.

"Physics Department, this is John speaking."

"Hello John, this is Melanie Moon. I'm trying to reach anyone who's working with the VLA."

108

"Hold on, let me transfer you."

As the on-hold music comes on, Melanie and I speak to each other briefly.

"It's odd that they are working on the weekend," Melanie says.

"It is weird. I really thought we were going to have to leave a message and Dr. Hamilton was going to force us to go down there," I say to Melanie.

The music abruptly stops.

"This is Scott Brinks with the VLA project. How may I help you?"

"Yes, my name is Melanie Moon. I'm a research assistant out of Richmond, Virginia and I'd like to inquire about a project you've been working on with my colleagues."

"What project?"

Melanie mutes the phone. "Should I tell him the name of the project?"

"You should do it. Let's just rip off the Band-Aid and see what happens."

Melanie unmutes the call and continues. "Project Lion's Tears."

There is a lengthy silence on the phone.

"Are you still there, Scott?"

"Yes, I'm here. Are you telling me that project is still active?" Scott asks, his voice tinged with nervousness.

This isn't sounding good. It already feels troubling when Gary tells me what he knows, but now I get the sense that Scott is about to confirm at least part of his story.

"Yes, it is," replies Melanie.

"Let me call you back." Scott then hangs up the phone.

Melanie and I look at each other nervously. While we don't have any idea why he hung up, we can't help but speculate. We're both too nervous to talk. Five minutes pass, and our phone starts to ring. It's a New Mexico number, but not from New Mexico Tech.

Melanie answers the phone and once again puts it on speaker. "Hello?"

"This is Scott. I'm calling you from another phone because I want to lessen the chances of this call being tracked." Scott speaks in a very low, cautious voice.

"Why are you concerned?"

"Because, Melanie, I don't want to disappear like the others."

Melanie and I look at each other wide eyed.

"Are you referring to the team that was working on Project Lion's Tears?" Melanie asks.

"No, I don't know what happened to that team. I'm referring to my colleagues here at New Mexico Tech. They disappeared about six months ago, and I'm told that they are sent to various space radios around the US."

"Interesting. Something tells me that you don't believe that explanation," says Melanie.

"I don't. My colleagues were working with the researchers from Project Lion's Tears, but I had no idea what they were looking for or why they were working such long hours. All I know is that they worked on the project until six months ago. Then, they are suddenly removed over a weekend. Since then, I'm the only civilian from New Mexico Tech still at the VLA, though my role is greatly reduced. I have no idea what they were doing until three weeks ago," responds Scott.

"What happened three weeks ago?" Melanie asks.

"While I'm in the break room, I stumble upon a thumb drive that's collecting dust. I'm doing some cleaning behind the fridge and that's where I find it. My curiosity is piqued, so I plug it into a laptop that I barely use. I discover so much information. I can't believe most of what I'm reading. It seems so unreal."

I mute the phone quickly and ask Melanie, "Can you ask him what the connection is with the VLA and Project Lion's Tears?"

"I was getting to that. Patience, Dr. Koraline."

Melanie unmutes the phone. "Scott, can you tell me what the connection is between this project and the VLA? Six months ago, my team in Richmond ended up taking over the project. However, we were given no information about what happened in New Mexico."

"You weren't told anything?" Scott asks, sounding surprised.

"Nothing. We came across some information this morning that opens our eyes some, but it still leaves us with so many questions," Melanie responds.

"Okay, I'll tell you what I've discovered. There are a ton of files, and I haven't gotten a chance to go through all of them. But I think what I've discovered should help you."

"Tell me what you know," says Melanie.

"Six months ago, the project manager is instructed by Washington to create a task force to investigate something going on at the VLA. Are you familiar with what happens when the aid takes Cody past the VLA?" he asks.

"Yes, we are aware," Melanie responds.

"Ok, I just want to make sure I didn't lose you on this next part. Something happens when the aid, Lauren, drives past the VLA. According to the staff on site, around the time Cody is near the VLA, a transmission is sent into deep space."

I mute the call once again. "Transmission? I thought the VLA could only receive signals," I say to Melanie.

"I'll ask him."

Melanie continues, "The VLA, from what I understand, can only receive signals, not send transmissions."

"Yes, that's true. However, we had built an experimental transmitter on site. But it wasn't fully operational. It wasn't even meant to be permanently installed on site. We're simply experimenting with it before it's sent to Montana. So, they're shocked to see a transmission of that strength is able to be sent. But it is. Two days after the transmission is sent, the VLA starts receiving a strong signal. At first, it's assumed that the signal is random and that we pick it up accidentally. However, no matter where the receivers are pointed, the signal is still being received. Something else that catches their attention is the type of signal it is. It is unlike anything the VLA has ever picked up. The signal is intelligible, and even more confusing, it is mostly in English! Four other deep space radios are picking up the same signal. A week passes and my colleagues are informed that Cody is having episodes. There is an assumption the episodes and the signal are connected."

"The signal, what is it saying?" Melanie asks.

'Do not intervene. Salus is at hand.'"

"You say the message is mostly in English. What isn't in English?" Melanie asks.

"Salus. They discovered that it's possible that Salus is Latin. Which, translated into English, is the word 'Salvation.' So, the message says, 'Do not interfere. Salvation is at hand,'" John replies.

That sounds incredibly ominous. What does it mean that salvation is at hand? The being says Salus is one of his many names. Does that mean he sees himself as the one who brings salvation? If so, what does he mean by salvation?

"Now that they have the signal, are they trying to determine its exact origin in space?" Melanie asks.

"Yes. But there are a few strange things they started to notice. Although they manage to identify a general area the signal is coming from, there is growing unease. The signal grows stronger on a daily basis, almost as if whatever it is has been getting closer to Earth. No one can make sense of it, and there are no clear answers. Then, three weeks after it begins, the signal abruptly stops. All the other radio telescopes stop detecting it as well. On the following day, all of my colleagues who have worked on the project are 'reassigned.' I'm genuinely worried that something may have happened to them," Scott says.

While we are talking, a crackling noise starts to come through. I think it's normal interference, but my gut is telling me that something is off. I think the call is being monitored! I quickly grab the phone out of Melanie's hand and end the call.

"What was that fo…" Before she can finish speaking, a loud knock hits the door. No one announces themselves. We are both terrified, unsure of what to do. I manage to pull myself together just enough to hide the MI6 laptop behind the bed. I barely get it there before the door bursts open with a violent kick. I don't know who these people are, but they are armed. They throw burlap bags over our heads and lead us out of the room.

Chapter 12

Catalyst

I cannot see anything. I'm terrified and have no idea if I am going to make it out of this alive. I hear car doors open, and we are led into a vehicle. The sacks are pulled off our heads, revealing a woman and a man sitting across from us. We are in some sort of extended vehicle. It does not seem like a limo, but I have no better way to describe it. I don't recognize either of them. They sit in silence, just staring at us.

The man is dressed in a blue polo shirt and jeans, carrying himself with a calm, professional demeanor. He has a deep brown complexion, with black hair and brown eyes. The woman wears a stylish blouse with jeans. She has red hair and blue eyes, the color of her eyes standing out sharply against her light complexion.

"Who are you and why are you kidnapping us?" Melanie asks.

"We are from the Department of Homeland Security," says the man.

"Did Secretary Jones send you?" I ask.

"No. I apologize for the manner of how we picked you up, but we knew if we identified ourselves that you would be hesitant to come with us," says the woman.

Melanie and I look at each other, confused.

"If Secretary Jones didn't send you, then why do you have us here?" Melanie asks.

"We have a major problem. First, let us introduce ourselves. I'm Matthew and this is my colleague, Carly. I'm about to inform you of some things that are taking place. We are aware that the two of you, along with the rest of your team, have been kept in the dark about Project Lion's Tears. The information was kept from you because the department was concerned that if everyone knew the truth about what happened in Socorro, the entire team might refuse to cooperate with us."

I'm filled with anger. I don't hold back. "Are we just disposable to you? Considering what happened in Socorro, it sure feels that way!" I don't know if Matthew and Carly are aware that I know what has taken place, but at this point, I'm too angry to care. Melanie gives me a worried look, her expression tense and uneasy. I can tell she is troubled by the possibility that they might already suspect we know the truth. It feels like she is afraid we have said too much too soon, and now there is no way to take it back.

"What she meant to say is what we speculate happened in Socorro," says Melanie.

"There's no need to hide it. We already know that you, along with Dr. Hamilton and Dr. Koraline, are aware. We intercepted Gary before he could leave town and persuaded him to tell us what he shared with you," Carly says.

"He was reluctant to tell us anything, but once we informed him of what was going on, he told us. The only thing he would not tell us is how he got in contact with you. However, due to the severity of the situation, that's not a concern we have now," says Matthew. "Secretary Jones will hate that I'm sharing this with you, but we are out of options. The reason why there's an urgency to get in contact with you is because we have lost all contact with Washington. Last night, my team was returning to headquarters from southern Virginia when we lost contact with them. We assumed that we were having phone signal problems, but the severity of the situation was made known to us when we attempted to drive into DC. Something or someone is preventing us from getting to DC. We made multiple attempts, but every time we tried, our vehicle was surrounded by a weird black and purple veil. Also, something strange would start happening to our vehicles. They would start to shake violently until we backed out of the veil. Then a voice out of nowhere would scream at us that we would face consequences if we proceeded any further."

"Salus is getting stronger every day!" I exclaim.

"Yes, he is. That is why we need your help. But first, I want to fill in the gaps in what you know with what we have. We were monitoring your calls, so we already know that contact was made with the being called Salus. We don't know what he is. He could be extraterrestrial or something else entirely. What we do know is that he is interested in Cody and in our planet. We have tried to figure out his motive or plan, but every attempt has failed. We brought you in hoping you might be able to unlock something hidden within Cody. We know Salus is trying to use his body, but we still don't know why or what his true intentions are," Carly says.

"I think there's something bigger going on here. I don't think Cody wanted this link; I think it was forced upon him," I respond.

"Dr. Koraline, please explain yourself," says Matthew.

"I recently had a dream that I believe came from Cody. He and Salus were both in it, and it seemed to show what really happened the day Cody was near the VLA. If the dream was a memory, then everything likely began with Lauren, the aid from the Socorro team. Gary said she passed the VLA by accident, but the dream suggested she went there on purpose to contact Salus. She told Cody she had a powerful and dangerous boss outside the facility who was interested in his abilities. I could not hear everything, but from what I gathered, she failed to reach him the first time but succeeded after they turned around at Datil. While she made contact near the VLA, Cody started screaming in pain. She did not seem bothered and continued driving afterward."

Matthew and Carly looked at each other. They shared a look of concern.

"This is horrifying. We had no idea that someone intentionally made contact. This changes everything. Do you have any indication that she was the only one? Do we know if there's more than one? This complicates things more than expected. We already knew not everyone could be trusted but this is a whole different level," says Carly.

"I understand what you're saying. We have to keep this information limited to a trusted few. But if Salus' powers are growing this quickly, there's a strong chance more veils will begin to appear. When they do, the media and the public are going to start demanding answers," said Matthew.

"As far as I know, Lauren is the only one. However, something tells me that there are more. I'm just curious to know why Salus would kill Lauren. I know we weren't there to see what exactly happened, but I refuse to believe that Cody did that."

"Dr. Koraline, what are you talking about?" asked Matthew.

"Which part?"

"About Lauren."

"What about her?" I ask.

"As far as we know, Lauren wasn't killed. We have no idea where she's at. She was kicked off from working directly on the project a week after she made that unauthorized trip. She was considered too much of a liability. We made her sign an NDA and then she was dismissed," says Carly. "Where did you hear that Lauren was dead?"

"He didn't know for sure since he couldn't get close enough to the facility, but Gary told me. As a matter of fact, he told me that the reason he didn't return to the facility was because he had a voicemail from Lauren telling him not to come back and it sounded like she was being attacked."

"Did Gary give any indication that she had been fired?" asked Matthew.

"No. He only said she was reprimanded and interrogated. I believe he said she was reduced to desk duty, too."

Matthew and Carly were looking concerned.

Melanie then speaks, "I take it by your facial expressions that either Gary is lying or Lauren may have had something to do with the team being killed. Or both."

Matthew pulls out his phone and makes a call. No one picked up. He tried again. Still no answer. "Carly, can you call Elizabeth and see if you can get her on your phone?"

"Yeah, I can."

Now Carly makes attempts, but she's not having any luck either. This isn't looking good at all. Matthew and Carly start to go into a panic. Matthew calls to the driver, "Change of plans! Head to the facility now!"

The driver takes a sharp right turn, which pushes me into Melanie, and speeds up. We have to be pushing ninety or ninety-five miles per hour.

"Why are we in such a hurry to get to the facility?" Melanie asks.

"Elizabeth, along with others, are with Gary. I wanted Elizabeth to bring Gary to a rendezvous point so we could interrogate him. Elizabeth isn't picking up," says Matthew.

"Okay, so she doesn't pick up. That doesn't mean that something happened, does it?" I ask.

"Not necessarily, but we do have a policy," Carly says. "If at least two people try to contact you and can't reach you after three attempts, we initiate a protocol of containment. That means we assume you may be compromised or in danger, and we begin restricting access, locking down communications, and isolating any sensitive information tied to you. Given how little we actually knew about this situation, we're not taking any chances."

That makes sense. I really would love to know if Gary is truly in on this. Because if he is, then there's no telling what lies he's told me. Melanie's phone starts to ring. It was Dr. Hamilton. She picks up the phone and puts it on speaker.

"Hello, Doctor."

"Melanie, where are you? Are you both okay?"

"Yes, we are. It's a bit of a long story," says Melanie.

"If you're referring to the Department of Homeland Security picking the two of you up, I already know. They arrived here at the facility, too."

"I see. We are on our way back to the facility with DHS people. We discovered some inconsistencies in the information Gary gave Dr. Koraline," says Melanie.

"Okay, well I'm glad both of you are on the way back. We have a major situation going on here. The entire facility is covered in that strange, black and purple veil. Everyone is outside except for Cody. We are not sure how to approach this," says Dr. Hamilton.

"Don't worry, Doctor, we will be there soon." Melanie ends the call.

"This is getting more dangerous by the hour," I say to the others.

"Well, Matthew, how do you want to handle this?" asks Carly.

Matthew sits there for a little bit, hand on his chin, trying to think of a plan.

"Here's what we will do. We will bring the two of you to the facility and we will continue making attempts to contact Elizabeth. In the meantime, Dr. Koraline, I think you need to make some type of contact with Cody. I don't want you to enter the building. Knowing what took place in Socorro, I don't want to unnecessarily lose lives. Do you think you can contact him from outside?" asks Matthew.

"I can try, but I'm not sure how," I reply. "Aside from the face-to-face contact I had, which ended being with Salus instead of Cody, the other way was through dreams," I say to Matthew.

"What if we did this? We have Dr. Koraline attempt to contact Cody from the outside. If that fails, we evacuate the facility and we take her back to her hotel room and have her fall asleep, and hopefully she can reach Cody in a dream without the influence of Salus," Carly suggests.

"We could do that. We can leave a couple of our staff to keep an eye on the facility from a distance and report anything else weird that is going on. We also need to coordinate with law enforcement to ensure this area is blocked off from the public. Are you tired, Dr. Koraline? Would you be able to fall asleep easily? If the first part of the plan doesn't work?" asks Matthew.

"I'm a little tired, but I'm not sure if I can fall asleep. I do have some melatonin that I had in my carry-on that I could use."

"Good. This is a very flimsy plan, but I'm not sure what else we can do," says Carly.

We soon arrive at the facility, and I can sense the darkness coming from inside before we even pull into the parking lot. Everyone is gathered at the edge of the lot, and we join them there.

Matthew and Carly fill Dr. Hamilton in on the plan, and he is not thrilled about me trying to contact Cody. However, he also admits that he is not sure what else they can do at this point.

"Good luck," Melanie says to me.

"Thanks."

I walk halfway across the parking lot and stop. I'm not even sure how I'm going to contact him, especially since I was face-to-face with him last time. Still, the veil seems to be growing, so there is a chance I can reach him from here. But I worry that I will not be able to connect with Cody at all and will end up speaking only to Salus.

"Cody, this is Dr. Koraline. May I talk to you?" There is no response. I try again. "Cody. This is very urgent. We need to talk and figure out what is going on."

Still nothing. I'm not sure what else to say. One idea crosses my mind, though it does not seem like the best one. But what choice do I have? Maybe it is the only way to reach Cody outside of my usual way of communicating with him.

"Salus, please let me talk to Cody."

The ground begins to shake slightly. At least I get a response this time, but I'm nervous.

"Geneva Koraline. Your attempt to contact Cody is in vain. Cody will soon be gone, and I'll have complete control of his body. There is nothing you can do to stop me."

A shockwave bursts from the building and knocks all of us to the ground. I get up and quickly run back to the others.

"I guess I need to make contact with him through dreaming," I say to the others.

"I do think that is our only option, but I'm concerned about the power he is able to exert," Matthew says. "The ground shaking and the shockwave happened just from inside the building. I fear he is only growing stronger. I will keep moving forward with my plan to get law enforcement to block off the area, but we may need military involvement."

"We need to at least inform the military and see if we can get the National Guard to assist law enforcement," Carly says. "But how are we going to reach the Pentagon? I know it is not in DC, but if we could not even get in contact with headquarters, we might not have any luck with the Pentagon either."

"Very true," Matthew replies.

"Dr. Koraline, I'll take you back to your hotel room. I'm going to have Melanie stay with you. With the amount of power he is showing, you may need someone close by in case something goes terribly wrong," Dr. Hamilton says.

"I appreciate that," I reply.

"Carly, Matthew, what do you want us to do in the meantime?" Dr. Hamilton asks.

"We are not sure what steps we need to take next. My recommendation is that you and your staff lay low for the time being. We will stay in communication, but I think we need to keep everyone away. This situation is too unstable for us to try anything outside of our plan. Dr. Koraline, please contact us immediately if you are successful and let us know what you find out," Matthew says.

"I will," I reply.

Melanie and I get into Dr. Hamilton's car, and he begins driving us to the hotel. About a minute after pulling out of the parking lot, Dr. Hamilton starts to speak.

"I'm not a fan of this plan. You have no backup or support while you are dreaming. What if something happens to you?"

"I have the same concerns. But even though Salus keeps telling me to leave this alone, he has not harmed me directly," I respond.

"I understand what you are saying. But there is no denying he is getting stronger. I don't think we can rely on past behavior to predict how he will react this time. Just promise me you will be careful and find a way to wake up if you feel like you are in danger," says Dr. Hamilton.

"I will do what I can."

The rest of the drive is quiet. When we reach the hotel, Melanie and I get out without saying anything else to Dr. Hamilton.

"Do you want me to get dinner? There is a chicken place a block over where I can grab something," Melanie says.

"Yeah, go ahead."

I'm not really hungry, but it gives me the time I need to contact Director Lynne. Melanie and Dr. Hamilton know I'm in contact with British Intelligence, but I would still prefer to reach out to Director Lynne without having to answer a bunch of questions. I'm not sure I'll have time to fill her in on everything, but I will try to give her a quick summary.

I make my way to my room and glance out the window to see when Melanie drives off. As soon as she pulls away, I grab the laptop wedged between the mattress and the bed frame and open it. Several missed messages from Director Lynne are waiting.

Dir_Lynne: How's it going?

Dir_Lynne: Are you ok?

Dir_Lynne: I'm really worried, it's been a while since you've contacted us.

There are ten other messages with similar wording expressing concern for me.

Dr_Kor: I don't have much time, so here are the key points. Gary gave me details about Socorro, but some may be false. A dream I had showed that an aid named Lauren deliberately took Cody near the VLA to contact a being she called her boss. After that, Cody began experiencing severe migraines. We believe this marked the start of his connection with the being, Salus. Most of the project staff died soon after, except for Gary and Lauren. Lauren had already been dismissed, though Gary failed to mention that. I later tried to speak to Cody but only reached Salus. DHS staff say they cannot contact Washington or enter the city without being warned off by Salus. Those are the main discoveries so far.

I see that Director Lynne sees the message, but she is not responding yet. In the meantime, I keep an eye on the window to watch for when Melanie returns, and then I hear a ping on the laptop. She messages me back.

Dir_Lynne: Thank you for getting us this information. It's not just those DHS employees who are having trouble reaching anyone in Washington. We are experiencing the same issue. We are also starting to hear from our NHS contacts that there's a rise in people reporting migraines and strange dreams. We knew there was a connection because everyone described hearing the same menacing voice saying, "Salus is coming." This brings major clarity to what is happening. However, I'm very concerned that people on another continent, with no connection to you, Cody, or this project, are experiencing these dreams. I believe something significant is about to happen. Thank you again for sharing this with us.

Chat ended.

I begin to feel a growing resolve to do whatever I can in the next dream. I know Salus is gaining power, but if people across the ocean are already feeling the effects, this could easily become a global catastrophe. Melanie returns with a bucket of fried chicken, mashed potatoes, and mac and cheese. We eat and make small talk about our backgrounds. I learn that Melanie was born in Utah but grew up all over the western United States. She has either lived in or visited nearly every state from Texas westward. She earned a bachelor's degree in photography from the Savannah College of

Art and Design. I think it is pretty neat that, even though she is from the western U.S., she went to school in my home state.

I wondered how she joined this project with just a photography degree. She explains that her main role is to document Cody's time at the facility with photographic evidence. I share a bit about my own background, earning my bachelor's from Georgia State University, my master's from the University of West Georgia, and my doctorate in psychology from Xavier University. I don't usually like going into my full academic history, but Melanie is persistent. I especially dislike being called "doctor." I prefer people to just call me Geneva or Koraline. I find out that she is asking because she is considering going back to school for a master's degree, though she is not sure in what field yet.

After dinner, I take a couple of melatonin and decide to try to sleep.

"I'm not sure how, but I'll try to be here for you in case you need me. Too bad I can't fall asleep at the same time as you so I can join you and help you," Melanie says.

"I'll be honest with you, Melanie, that would be really neat if it were possible. Who knows? I do think you should get some sleep, but also keep your guard up. I just remembered that Gary met me at this hotel, and with everything going on and the fact that they couldn't reach Elizabeth, I think we should be careful. I wish I had asked Carly and Matthew to send someone to keep watch," I say to Melanie.

"I don't think Gary would be dumb to come back here. But we really don't know what he is up to. There's something I've been thinking about, and I wasn't sure if I should say it," Melanie says.

"What is it?" I ask.

"We automatically assumed Gary is lying. But has anyone stopped to think that maybe DHS is lying to us about Lauren? I mean, we don't really know Gary, but DHS has not exactly been honest with us either," she says.

She makes a really good point.

"You're right. We really are taking a gamble. I don't trust DHS completely either, but I feel like this group actually wants to help. I don't know if that is just my gut or if I'm being naïve. Either way, Cody is the one who knows the truth, and I intend to find it," I respond.

"I agree about Cody. Just be careful, Doctor."

I head into the bathroom to get ready for bed. While getting ready, I feel something in my pocket. I don't remember putting anything there besides my phone. I reach in and, to my shock, pull out another key. This one has a lion's head, with its mane surrounded by a thick, beautifully designed circle.

I try to figure out when I could have gotten it. Maybe when I was face-to-face with Salus, or when I tried to contact him outside the facility. But that does not make sense. Why would he give me a key? Maybe I had it after the last dream and just never noticed it while I was focused on everything Gary told me and what I saw.

Either way, I hope this key will help me in the next dream. Maybe the chest will appear again. I place the key back in my pocket and crawl into bed.

Melanie is sitting on the other bed. "Goodnight, Dr. Koraline."

"Goodnight, Melanie."

I drift off to sleep quickly, having done everything I can to prepare for what comes next.

Chapter 13

Call for Help

The Fifth Dream

As the dream begins, I find myself in the middle of an ocean. I'm sitting in a canoe with an oar inside the boat. The ocean isn't calm. Huge waves are crashing around me, and it looks like a storm is coming. I start to feel a little seasick. I cannot see land anywhere and I have no idea which direction to row, so I decide to start paddling in the direction the canoe is already facing. I have noticed that in these dreams, what I'm searching for usually finds a way to me, so I figure the direction does not matter.

Rowing is difficult. The waves crash against me again and again, leaving me completely soaked. I keep my focus on what I'm trying to find, Cody and the treasure chest from the last dream. I also know there is a good chance I'll encounter Salus, especially now that his power seems to be growing. I just hope I can find Cody and the chest before he appears. If I can wake up before he reaches me, that would be ideal.

The farther I travel, the more seasick I feel. Soon, I notice something strange in the water, a buoy in the distance. At first, it looks ordinary, but then I see the light on it is shaped like the key I recently found. The lion's head glows red, and it sends a chill through me. I hope this is where the chest is hidden.

I push forward, but each stroke gets slower. My arms ache, and my legs feel like they are dragging weights. The buoy bobs in the distance, always just out of reach. No matter how hard I row, it seems to drift farther away. Maybe it's just my fatigue. Eventually, I reach it, my muscles burning and chest tight as if I'd been rowing for hours.

The space around the buoy is strangely calm. It feels like something is protecting it from the waves. I search all around it, but I do not see the chest. Something tells me it is not going to be that easy. I have no idea what to do next. There are no other buoys in sight.

As I'm about to give up, I hear Cody's faint voice.

"Cody, what are you trying to tell me? I hear you, but you are unclear."

He speaks again, a little louder, but I still cannot make out what he is saying. I want to tell him to speak up, but then I realize this is the first time I'm hearing his voice without seeing him. That is not a good sign. It might mean Salus is close to completely pushing him out. Based on my previous interactions with Salus, that appears to be the case.

"Okay, Cody, I know you might be scared. I don't blame you. I'm not asking you to expose yourself, but I need you to speak a little more clearly so I can understand you."

He speaks again, and this time I understand. "The buoy is anchored to it."

He must mean the chest. That has to be it. But how am I supposed to reach it? I don't have any gear to go underwater. Then I remember something. Chris, one of the embassy staffers who drove me in London, told me about a dream where he felt like he was underwater but could breathe. I know dreams don't always follow logic, but the idea of going underwater without gear still scares me. What if that breathing ability only applied to his dream?

Still, I know I need to try. I decide to take a leap of faith.

Using the buoy to balance myself, I stand up in the canoe and count to three. One. Two. Three. No turning back now.

I jump in feet first, expecting either to drown or to find myself in a dream version of an underwater scene like Chris described. But I am wrong. As soon as I hit the surface, I begin to fall. There is no water around me anymore. It's like I have entered another world. I look up and can still see the surface above me. I have no idea where this is going to lead.

While falling, I manage to orient myself and observe a long chain beneath me. I assume it is connected to the chest. The whole environment around me is pure white. It reminds me of the first dream I had with Cody. The air feels thick. Each breath heavier than the last.

I look down and see the chest.

My body slows as I approach it, until I'm able to land softly on my feet. I pull the key from my pocket and crouch down at the chest. I insert the key and hear a series of internal locks clicking open.

As the final lock shifts, I find myself in a room. I don't recognize it. It doesn't look like the facility in Richmond or anywhere I've been before. It looks like some kind of breakroom. There is a window, so I go to look outside. I don't recognize the landscape or any of the buildings. But in the distance, I spot a building with a flagpole. I see the American flag and a yellowish state flag flying beside it. That is the flag of New Mexico. I must be in Socorro. This must be the space they used when they had Cody here. Maybe I can find some answers.

I leave the room and begin to explore the rest of the building. Every now and then, I pass someone walking to or from different parts of the facility. As I explore, I find myself standing outside a room. The door is closed and unmarked, but I have this strange feeling that this is where I'm supposed to go. I wait outside the door and hear someone begging to be allowed to sleep. The voice sounds desperate, filled with weeping and pleading for help.

I decide to enter the room, and I cannot believe what I see. It is Cody, but he looks sleep-deprived and thin. I'm confused about what is happening, but I assume this must be when Salus first became a part of him. I feel horrible for Cody. I want to know why Salus is putting him through this. It makes me angry, and I want to step in, but I remind myself this is just a memory.

I look around the room and recognize only one person. Lauren. I want to confront her for causing all of this. But then she starts to speak, and I listen.

"Do you think he has had enough? We have deprived him of sleep for three days and food for two. This is too much."

"Lauren, you are lucky we are even allowing you in here. Know your place, or you will not be back."

132

Lauren goes silent, unable to meet Cody's eyes. I see the compassion in her expression as her eyes begin to fill with tears. It looks like she has formed a bond with him and truly cares about him.

I'm not sure what they are doing in this room. I see people with clipboards and others monitoring equipment. Lauren still looks ashamed and uncomfortable.

"Lauren, do you still need to pick up the package for work tomorrow?" one of the researchers asks.

"Yes, I do," she replies.

"Okay, you can pick it up tomorrow before work. Just make sure you take care of it before you pick up Cody."

"I know the protocol. No need to remind me."

Something feels off. Is this before Lauren took Cody to the VLA? I'm struggling to understand what is happening. If this is before she made contact with Salus, then what is going on right now?

"They were under pressure," Cody's voice says, but not from his body.

"Cody, what is happening to you? What do you mean, under pressure?" I ask.

"The first two years of this project led nowhere. I tried to do everything they asked, answered all their questions, completed every evaluation, but they kept hitting dead ends. Six months ago, Washington got tired of the lack of progress. They were not satisfied with the methods the team was using, so they sent four new researchers to change everything. The remaining staff protested, but the new team introduced harsh methods. They started depriving me of sleep, cutting my food, and watching how it affected my dreams and how I influenced the dreams of others. They seemed more intent on stopping me than understanding me. I still don't know why I have this ability. I cannot control it. Sometimes they would shock me when they saw brain activity that showed I was dreaming," Cody says.

"How could they do this to you? Was everyone okay with this?" I ask.

"It wasn't popular. At first, the four new staff worked with the rest of the team, but when people pushed back, they were threatened. Their jobs and families were used against them. Lauren was the only one who stood up for me."

I'm stunned. I feel terrible for judging Lauren too harshly. This changes everything I thought about her. Still, it raises more questions. Was Lauren trying to save Cody? Or is she part of something bigger? One thing is certain, I need to find her and talk to her. Now I understand why Washington kept this from me and the team in Richmond. The project took a dark turn. What started as research became abuse. They should be ashamed.

The entire environment turns white and stays that way for ten seconds. As the white environment begins to fade, I find myself back in the same room I was in when I first entered this memory. It doesn't take long to understand why I'm here. I start to hear people yelling and screaming. I run out of the room and immediately see the cause of the panic. It is Salus. He towers above everyone and appears in what I consider the closest thing to his human form, the same form I saw in a previous dream. People are trying to escape the building, but they cannot get out. They rush to another exit, but they are still unsuccessful.

"Why can't we open the door? Did someone block the outside?" someone asks. I cannot tell who said it. I go to the door, and to my surprise, I'm able to walk through it. I end up at the back of the building, face to face with someone I never expected to see. It's Lauren. I soon realize she is going from door to door, blocking them with heavy materials. I assume she is doing this at every exit. After stacking the materials, she extends her hands. Slowly, everything begins to shimmer with the same veil I saw back at the facility in Richmond. I'm in shock and disbelief. I want to know more about Lauren and her connection to all of this. I want to follow her, but I also need to see what happened inside the facility that day.

I head back inside and find all the staff gathered in a room near the center of the building. I make my way to it. Everyone inside is tense and nervous. I hear snippets of conversation as people whisper in confusion.

"Who is that person? I've never seen anyone like this before."

"Why is he doing this?"

"Has this person been inside Cody the whole time?"

Everyone is confused and trying to figure out how to escape. It doesn't take long for Salus to find them. He tears the door off and enters the room. He looks up to the sky and raises his arms. A black and purple veil pours out from him, the same one I saw before. It fills the room completely. The space that was filled with shouting just moments ago falls silent. When the veil clears, everyone in the room is lying dead on the floor. My breath catches. The room is still. Lifeless bodies cover the floor, their eyes frozen in fear. I stagger back, a wave of nausea rising in my throat. This is not just a memory. It's a warning.

Salus stands there, unmoving. I don't understand why he just stands there, until I realize he can see me.

"Dr. Koraline, you certainly are a stubborn one. No matter how many times I tell you not to get involved, you keep digging deeper," Salus says.

"Why do you not want me involved? It also doesn't help your case that you have not explained your intentions, your interest in Cody, or why you killed all these people. Everything you do only pushes me to get more involved," I reply.

Salus looks away for a moment. I think I understand what he wants now, especially after seeing that. But I don't want to let him know that. I have no idea how he might react to me being here.

"My intentions are none of your concern. I'm simply doing what I must. As for you, if you keep interfering, I'll deal with you sooner rather than later," he says.

What does he mean by that? Is he after me too? That is when I start putting the pieces together. This may be a mission of revenge. Salus could be targeting the people who hurt Cody. If he has been inside Cody, he would know everything Cody experienced, and he might have felt it himself. If that is true, then I'm likely a target too, since I unintentionally started all of this. It's terrifying, but I am also glad that some of this is beginning to make sense.

One question still lingers.

"Why are you doing this? I think I may understand a little of your intention. What is your connection to Cody?"

"None of your concern!" he shouts.

Then I hear Cody's voice. It is a whisper. "Run."

136

He doesn't have to say it twice. I bolt. My feet pound the ground as I sprint into the darkness, my breath catching in my throat. After a few seconds, I realize something is wrong.

There are no footsteps behind me. Only mine. I glance over my shoulder and freeze.

Salus has stopped. He stands perfectly still, just a dark shape in the distance. Then, slowly and deliberately, he raises his arms and stretches them toward me.

The air shifts.

A dark veil erupts from his hands, spreading outward like heavy smoke, swallowing everything in its path. Before I can move, it wraps around me like a living thing, tightening, gripping, paralyzing. I cannot move. Not even to scream. My body is frozen, but my mind screams. Every instinct urges me to run, to fight, to do something, but I'm trapped, helpless inside the veil.

Salus begins walking toward me, calm and steady. His red eyes lock onto mine, burning with something ancient and merciless. He stops just inches from my face. Slowly, he opens his mouth slightly, as if he is about to speak.

But before a sound escapes, I wake up. My heart is racing. I'm drenched in sweat. The echo of his presence still lingers in my chest like smoke.

As I wake up, I see that it's morning. Melanie is already awake and runs over to me.

"Dr. Koraline, glad to see that you're awake. How did it go?"

"Melanie, I want to tell you everything, but I need some time to process it first. When I brief the others, you'll hear it then. Hopefully by that point, I'll be ready to explain what happened," I reply.

"No offense, Doctor, but everything you've discovered already changes things. How is this any different?"

"Because, Melanie, for the first time since learning about all of this, I feel as if my life, and the lives of everyone involved with this project, are in grave danger."

Melanie is taken aback.

"Well, given the information that we learned about what happened in Socorro and what happened yesterday, I think many of us already felt that we were in danger," says Melanie.

"I understand what you're saying, Melanie, but this time I'm certain we are in real danger. What happened in Socorro was not random. It was an act of revenge against the team."

Melanie turns pale. She now realizes the seriousness of what has been revealed to me.

"I see. I'm sorry for trying to push you for information. What you saw sounds very intense from the little you're telling me. How soon do you want to meet with Dr. Hamilton and the others? Do you think an hour is enough time to get your thoughts together?"

I nod my head yes.

"Okay, it's 7:30 right now. I'll shoot a text to Dr. Hamilton for all of us to meet at 9:30. We can leave here at 9. Does that work for you?" asks Melanie.

"Yes. That'll be fine," I respond.

"Okay, I'll set it up." Melanie hops on her phone and starts getting everything set up for the day.

I know Director Lynne will be expecting me to contact her soon. However, I'm not too worried about keeping her informed at the moment. Everyone's safety, including my own, has now become my top priority. I'll fill her in later today. She's definitely in for a shock.

Chapter 14

NEW PLAN

Nine o'clock is here before we know it. I barely finish breakfast in time, as my mind is preoccupied with trying to understand everything I witnessed in that dream. When I go back to my room, I see a couple of suitcases by my door. I was confused until I remember that I was still waiting on luggage from the diversion. So much has been happening these past few days that I completely forgot I was still waiting on this stuff. Besides the fresh clothes, I don't think my luggage is going to be much help to me with this situation. I quickly put my suitcases in my room and meet Melanie at her car. She already has the car started and is waiting for me.

"Okay, Doctor, here's what we are about to do. For obvious reasons, we're not going to the facility as there hasn't been any change from what we saw yesterday. Even if there was, no one is wanting to risk being near Cody right now. We are going to be meeting at Dr. Hamilton's house which is located twenty miles south of here. This meeting includes us, Dr. Hamilton, and

Matthew and Carly from DHS. Dr. Hamilton preferred not to involve other staff unless needed," says Melanie.

"Sounds good. I'm glad that Matthew and Carly are going to be there. I have some serious questions I need to ask them. I'm hoping I can get my questions out before I blow up in a rage at them," I say to Melanie.

"Wow. You said I'd hear about the dream once we meet with everyone, but now I'm really starting to worry about whatever it is you saw," Melanie says.

"I know. Again, I'm really sorry for keeping you in the dark. However, when you hear what I have to say, I think you'll understand why I needed some time to think on this," I respond.

"I trust you. I just hate waiting. Especially with everything that's been going on. My anxiety is through the roof," Melanie says.

"You can have music playing, though. That may even help me out more."

Melanie puts her music on shuffle, and we start to make our way to Dr. Hamilton's house. I really do feel bad for Melanie. I'm sure she's probably thinking that I don't trust her. Which isn't the case at all. I just want to make sure that I actually saw and heard what I witnessed so I can be better prepared for everyone's questions.

We arrive at Dr. Hamilton's house, which is a ranch-style residence located in a remote area. Looking at the vehicles parked outside, it appears that we're the last ones to arrive. Dr. Hamilton opens the door and welcomes us in. He offers us coffee, which I'm not going to refuse. I need more caffeine today.

The living room is immediately to the left after coming through the door. We see Matthew and Carly sipping on their coffee and sitting on the couch. I sit in one of the recliners that faces the other couches and decide to have some conversation while I'm waiting on my coffee.

"Any updates from the facility?" I ask.

"Nothing has changed so far," responds Carly.

"How about your colleague, Elizabeth? Have you heard anything from her?" Melanie asks.

"We did. She says that she's going to meet us here shortly to talk about what happened to her and the others. I tried to get her to tell me over the phone, but she insisted on only telling me in person," says Matthew. "How did it go last night? Were you able to get more information?"

"Oh, yes. I got answers, and I definitely have questions for the two of you," I respond angrily.

Matthew and Carly exchange a quick glance, their expressions tightening. They say nothing, but the way they shift uneasily tells me they hadn't expected my anger. They are not sure how to respond to it.

Dr. Hamilton comes in with my coffee.

"Here you go. They took the rest of the cream and sugar, so I hope you like black coffee."

"That works well for me. I prefer my coffee black," I reply.

"Okay, Dr. Koraline, why don't you fill us in on what you find out in your dream?" says Dr. Hamilton.

"I find out some very disturbing things. I saw what happened to everyone working in Socorro. But before that, I saw what happens weeks earlier. More specifically, the day before Lauren takes Cody to the VLA. What I saw on that day is horrific. The DHS has a lot of explaining to do."

142

Matthew and Carly look confused and glance at each other.

I tell them that six months before it all falls apart, Washington brings in new researchers who deprive Cody of sleep and food. I explain how Lauren tries to advocate for him but is ignored. Matthew and Carly look horrified when I describe the massacre and how it seems like an act of revenge. I also can't leave out that Lauren helps block the exits, trapping the staff inside. It's not my place to decide what's justified, but at least now we understand where it all started.

Matthew and Carly exchange a tense glance. Carly's eyes drop to the floor, and Matthew shifts uncomfortably in his seat. I want to believe their body language, but after all the lies their organization has told, it's hard to trust a single word they say.

"We're told that everyone died because Cody's abilities got out of control. I'm really at a loss for words right now," says Matthew.

I look at Carly and notice that she's growing visibly angry. Still upset with DHS, my frustration gets the best of me and I say something ugly to Carly.

"What's wrong, Carly? Are you upset that all of you got exposed for what was truly happening with Cody?"

Carly finally speaks up. "No! How dare you insinuate this? Do you want to know why I'm angry? I'll tell you why! You may have been lied to, but I was lied to first. I oversaw this project for the first two years. I visited the facility every two months to check up on things and see how Cody is doing. But after two years, Secretary Jones removes me from the position and the project. When I ask him why, he simply tells me that two years is a long time to be on one assignment with little results. I try to explain that figuring out whatever Cody has will take time because it's beyond our current understanding. He tells me he understands and has me write a full report for the next person to follow. I stress how important it is to treat Cody with care. Later, I get reassigned when Cody is moved to Richmond and work with Matthew. I trusted Secretary Jones and believed him when he says nothing has changed. So, hearing this now, and realizing why I was really removed, makes me furious. Don't you ever question my commitment to treating him fairly!"

"I'm sorry for letting my anger get the best of me and accusing you of wrongdoing, Carly. I'm just tired and frustrated that I keep finding out the truth through dreams instead of through people," I respond.

"I understand your frustration, I really do. But I can't accept your apology right now. That accusation was personal," responds Carly.

I decide it's best to leave the conversation alone. I know I crossed a line with what I said, but part of me doesn't regret it. I doubt Carly would have revealed any of that if I didn't push her. If she is being honest, then Secretary Jones and possibly others close to him know far more than they have let on. It also makes me think more clearly about what might be unfolding in Washington. If the massacre was an act of revenge, then something even worse could be heading there next.

There's a silence in the room after our exchange. I think everyone is now afraid to speak as we sip our drinks and stare off into space.

"Considering everything we now know about what's been taking place," starts Melanie, "I think it's in our best interest to operate outside of DHS headquarters supervision. Yes, I'm even referring to both of you." She looks at Matthew and Carly.

Dr. Hamilton speaks. "I agree with Melanie. I think we should continue using my house as our operating base."

"I agree. We're starting to see how deep the rabbit hole goes. I think we should contact the rest of the staff and tell them not to return to the Richmond facility until further notice. We can't risk putting more lives in danger," says Matthew.

Before Matthew could continue, the doorbell rings. Dr. Hamilton pulls up his doorbell camera, then turns the phone toward us and asks if we know who it is.

We see a woman standing at the doorstep, dressed in a tailored dark suit that gives off an unmistakably professional vibe. Her dark hair is pulled back neatly, and though her expression is composed, there's a sharpness in her eyes that hints she isn't here for small talk. Even through the phone, she radiates authority and purpose.

"Oh! That's Elizabeth!" says Matthew. He gets up and lets her in. They come into the living room, and Elizabeth looks winded.

"Okay, Elizabeth, what's so urgent and important that you couldn't tell us over the phone?" asks Carly.

"It's Gary. He's been taken," responds Elizabeth.

"Taken? By who?" I ask.

"We don't know. We went to our rendezvous point, which is at a warehouse. I went into another part of the warehouse to look for our bottled water, and when I came back, everyone that was watching him had been knocked out unconscious. I started checking on everyone, and I found a note in one of our staff member's hands. I grabbed the note, looked at it, and then put it in my pocket. As soon as I put it in my pocket, a woman came out of nowhere and extended her hands toward me. That strange veil came from her hands, and suddenly I was somewhere completely unfamiliar. For a moment, I thought I had been transported to another world," says Elizabeth. "The environment seemed otherworldly. It was white everywhere, and I couldn't get a sense if I was in a room or outside."

This sounds like my first dream.

Elizabeth continues, "When I woke up, I realized she had somehow placed me into a dream. While I was dreaming, I saw a child in an orange onesie. I didn't recognize him, and he never said a word. He simply looked at me and handed me this."

Elizabeth reaches into her pocket and pulls out a key. I see that it has the same antique appearance as the other two keys I've received. This one has a horse's head at the top, identical to the one on the chest. What surprises me is that someone else has received a key. I didn't even think to check my own pockets this morning to see if I brought one back from my dream.

"I have no idea what this key is for, and what confuses me even more is why it was given to me. I don't understand how I woke up from that dream with it in my pocket. Can someone please explain what is happening? Is Cody really capable of all this?"

"I can explain the key. In the dreams that I've been having recently, a huge chest has appeared. The chest has four keyholes, and above each keyhole there's a different symbol. The first one is an owl, the second one is a lion, the third one is a horse, and the fourth one is a pocket watch. I've unlocked the first two locks. Every time I unlock a lock, I end up in a memory of Cody's. They have revealed plenty of information. This is where I found out about Lauren and also about the secrets that were kept from us in Socorro. I'm sorry I haven't told you all about the keys and the chest. I wasn't expecting someone else to get a key. Also, I was still having trouble processing whether I was imagining this or not," I say.

"Dr. Koraline, I do wish that you had told us this sooner. However, I can understand why you didn't. There's been so much strange stuff happening around Cody that cannot be explained. I'm just thankful that you told us what you found out each time you opened a lock," says Carly.

"What was the note you had?" asks Dr. Hamilton.

She pulls out the note from her pocket and hands it to me. "It was for you."

For me? I definitely don't expect that. I open the note.

Doctor, you'll find answers at T. My suspicions were right.

-Gary

I read the note aloud. From the way everyone reacts, it seems like they pick up on my confusion. It's as if they know I'm just as lost as they are about the meaning.

"Travel to T. Does T mean anything to any of you?" I ask.

"Not to me," says Melanie.

The rest follow suit, saying they don't know what it means.

"What suspicions is he referring to?" asks Matthew.

"I have no idea. I didn't even know he was looking into anything. I got the sense that he was trying to put this behind him and move on," I respond. "When did he write this? Do you think he had it the whole time?"

"I think it was before he was taken. He wouldn't talk to us when we asked him questions about his connection to Lauren. He only asked for a piece of paper, wrote something on it, and stuffed it in his pocket. He refused to give us the note," says Elizabeth.

I'm not sure what to think of this.

"Do you think T could be referring to something connected to him?" asks Melanie. "Maybe there's a town connected to him that starts with a T."

"That's it!" I exclaim.

Everyone looks at me.

"It has to be Torrington! Torrington, Wyoming! He went there to try and keep a low profile after what happened in Socorro," I say to the rest of the group.

"Torrington? Why there? Does he have family or friends there?" asks Melanie.

"No, he said he chose it blindly," I responded.

"That's wild! I actually graduated high school in Torrington," says Melanie.

"No way! What are the chances you lived in the same town Gary ended up moving to?" Matthew replies.

"It is crazy. Torrington is such an out-of-the-way town that I'm just surprised that of all places he could've relocate to, he chose there," says Melanie.

"Melanie, what's the closest airport to Torrington?" asks Carly.

"Well, if you're not concerned about the size of the airport, the closest airport is in Scottsbluff, Nebraska. There's also one in Cheyenne, Wyoming," responds Melanie.

I see Matthew furiously typing and scrolling on his phone. I wonder if he's looking up flights to get out there.

"Alright, it looks like both airports require a connection through Denver. I was going to suggest flying you out of Richmond and then connecting to Scottsbluff or Cheyenne, but those flights are sold out. So instead, I say we fly you to Denver and drive the rest of the way to Torrington," says Matthew.

"Okay, thank you. We need to follow every lead we can get to put all the pieces together," I mention to the others.

"I agree. Also, since Melanie has lived in Torrington, I suggest she go with you," says Dr. Hamilton.

"I agree. Not only because she knows the area. I also don't feel comfortable with you going by yourself. The two of you go there and see what you can find. Do we know his address?" says Carly.

"I'm afraid we don't. We are going to have to do some research before we head out," says Melanie.

Matthew gets out his wallet and hands Melanie a credit card. "Here you go. This is a credit card connected with DHS. Use it to purchase airline tickets, rental cars, and anything else you need. Just don't go too crazy with it and please keep all of your receipts. I must turn in an expense report every month. We are not allowed to give cards to non-DHS employees, but these are extraordinary circumstances. Dr. Hamilton, I'm going to use your printer. I'm going to print out special orders for them so they can use the card if they are questioned. Also, you can use your badges that you both received to get into the facility. They both say 'Department of Homeland Security' so hopefully that'll be enough to get you past some barriers."

"Thank you. We'll go there and hopefully return as soon as we possibly can," I say to Matthew.

"You're welcome. Melanie, go to your house and grab what you need in case you need to stay longer than a day. Same with you, Dr. Koraline," says Matthew.

"Will do," I say.

Melanie and I get up, and before we head to the car, Carly gives us a business card that has both hers and Matthew's numbers on it. Melanie puts their information on the burner phone while we head to her car. We decide she'll drop me off at my hotel first, since it's on the way to her house. She lives north of Richmond, so it makes sense. Melanie spends the drive thinking out loud about what she needs to bring with her. We eventually arrive at my hotel, and before I get out, I decide to ask her a question about our trip.

"How are we going to find where he lives?"

"I have a friend who still lives there and manages an apartment complex. He might be one of her tenants, but even if he's not, I'm hoping she can point us in the right direction," says Melanie. "The landlords and landladies in that area are pretty close, so I'm counting on her to ask around and see what she can dig up."

"That's good. He could've stayed anywhere. Though, while an apartment seems logical, if he's trying to keep a low profile, he may have stayed at a motel," I suggest.

"Good point, but even with most hotels, you need a government ID in order to reserve a room," Melanie says.

"While that is true, I do imagine that some places may look the other way if you give them enough money upfront," I reply.

"True. Well, I'll call her on the way to my house and see if I can find out anything from her," says Melanie.

"Okay, see you soon."

I get out of the car and head to my room. I wish I had a way to find where he lived. Then a thought comes to mind. I could ask Director Lynne. Maybe they pinged his IP address when he contacted her. I'm not completely sure if this is a good idea or not, but I figure I'll try it anyway.

I get out the MI6 laptop and send Director Lynne a chat:

Dr_Kor: Question, when Gary made contact with you, did MI6 ping his IP address?

I notice that she isn't online, which is a first. I think I've gotten spoiled by her instant replies. I leave the laptop open and pack my carry-on with a few clothes and some toiletries that don't need to be checked in. I sit on the bed and play on my phone for about thirty minutes. Still no response from Director Lynne. Melanie texts me and says she's five minutes out. I continue waiting for a response; still nothing. I go ahead and close the laptop and pack it in my carry-on.

Even though I have the laptop packed already, I'm still expecting to hear the ping from the chat service. Melanie gets to the hotel, and I meet her at her car. She informs me that she got us a flight that leaves Richmond in three hours, 3:50 PM to be exact. We're scheduled to arrive in Denver around 5:50 local time, making it roughly a four-hour flight. The drive to the airport is quiet. I can tell we're both uneasy about this assignment. It's unfamiliar territory, this is outside our usual professional experience.

I find myself wondering why Matthew or Carly aren't the ones going instead of us. Maybe they want me as far from Salus as possible. I wouldn't be surprised if they're hoping that distance might weaken his influence. But that feels foolish to me. Salus has grown into something far beyond what distance alone can control. Still, even with all the nerves, Melanie and I are committed. I just hope our determination will be enough.

Chapter 15

More Questions than Answers

We make our way to the airport. On the way, we discuss various things. I tell Melanie that I asked MI6 if they pinged Gary's IP address when he made contact with them, but I haven't received a response yet. Melanie informs me that her apartment manager friend, Juliet, is going to see what she can find out for us. She doesn't have a Gary listed as one of her tenants, but she's checking with other property owners. So far, our leads are coming up short, but we're hoping that by the time we reach Denver, there will at least be some small developments.

We make it through security and find seats at our gate. While we wait, I decide to ask Melanie about Torrington.

"How is Torrington? How did you like living there?"

Melanie responds, "You know, it's been years since I lived in Torrington. It was such a small town, but I have a lot of memories from there. As you know, we moved around so much when I was a kid. Torrington was one of the few places where I had some roots planted. I used to work at Hardee's. It was one of my first jobs. I also worked at this little hotel called King's Inn. It wasn't anything fancy, but the people I met there made it interesting. There was a theater in town, too. It wasn't big, but we all used to go there, especially on weekends. So many good memories from that place. My dad and I had this routine where we'd stop by Smoker Friendly, which was a convenience store. We'd pick up snacks or whatever we needed. It wasn't anything special, but those little moments always stuck with me. I used to love spending time at Pioneer Park, too. I'd go there just to relax, maybe play disc golf or walk around. One time, our dog even found a guinea pig there! I have no idea how it got there, but it was the most random thing. We took the guinea pig home, and I was happy that I had a new pet. Torrington is a small, simple town, but I do miss it on occasion."

"Sounds like a neat little town. Never heard of that town before Gary. To be quite honest, Wyoming is a state that I barely think about. I have considered taking a trip to Yellowstone National Park. Is that close to Torrington?"

"Yellowstone is at the opposite end of the state. Torrington is closer to Nebraska than it is to Yellowstone," Melanie responds. "Why don't you tell me a little bit about where you're from?"

"I grew up in the once small city of Douglasville, Georgia. It was a somewhat quiet town until they opened up a mall in the 90s. Ever since then, the city just kept growing. I haven't lived in Douglasville in a very long time, but every time I visit, there's always some new housing or business being built somewhere in the city or county," I say.

"Definitely sounds more crowded than Torrington!" Melanie says.

"Yeah, it doesn't help that it's not very far from Atlanta and that city just keeps on growing, too. Don't know if I really want to ever move back, to be honest. How about you? Would you ever move back to Torrington?" I ask.

"I don't see myself moving back. Am I saying it'll never happen? No. However, realistically, I don't see myself going back to Wyoming to live."

We continue talking about our childhoods and some of our similarities and differences. I was raised by a single mom; she was raised by a single dad. I lived in one state for my entire childhood; she lived in almost every state from Texas westward. We talk a little bit about some of our favorite TV shows and things we like to do in our free time. The two of us eventually run out of things to say and spend the rest of our time on our phones while we wait to board.

We have about twenty minutes before boarding starts, so I decide to quickly use the bathroom. On my way back to the waiting area, I overhear a phone conversation with someone who I assume is an airport employee.

"The flights to Denver, Atlanta, and Houston will be allowed to take off. After they take off, the FAA will order a ground stop at our airport. I don't have full details as to why this order has come down."

Ground stop? That makes me a little nervous about getting onto our flight. I'd love to know why they are planning a ground stop at this airport. I'm also concerned why they're letting our flight, along with a couple of others, take off before they put this ground stop into effect.

I text Melanie and tell her what I just heard. She texts back a few minutes later and says she can't find anything in the news to explain what's going on. Melanie suggests that maybe there are storms in the area. We don't know for sure, though we start discussing whether or not we want to get on this flight. We both come to the consensus that we should risk it. We need to get to Wyoming as fast as possible, and if this ground stop happens, it's only going to put us even further behind.

The boarding process begins. We wait for our zone in the main cabin to be called up. While we wait, I suddenly worry about falling asleep on the plane. I'm concerned about having one of these dreams in such a confined space, especially knowing that Salus's power keeps growing. I don't really have much time to fully think through all the possibilities. That's probably for the best; I don't want to work myself up more than I already am.

We eventually board our flight and get situated. Word starts to spread that this is one of the last flights leaving Richmond Airport. Melanie and I glance at each other, wondering if we can find more information now that more people are catching on. She quickly pulls out her phone and starts searching; there's nothing new. Just a couple of local stations reporting that a ground stop is coming to Richmond, but still no official reason. We're concerned that this might be connected to Salus.

"Let's just hope that nothing happens during our flight," I say to Melanie.

"I'm hoping for the same. I'm also hoping there's nothing weird going on at the other airports," she responds.

We both put in our wireless headphones and start playing music. I go with my favorite playlist, "2000s Throwback" on

Spotify. I notice it doesn't take long for us to start taxiing to the runway. They're really trying to push us out of here. I plan to stay awake as long as I can, but I know myself. I'll probably be falling asleep soon.

Great. My eyes are already starting to drift. I see that Melanie is also struggling to stay awake. I was so nervous that I completely forgot to grab coffee or an energy drink. I do my best to hold out until the beverage service starts so I can finally get some caffeine.

About twenty minutes later, the flight attendants begin the beverage service. When they reach my row, I ask for a cup of coffee, hoping it's strong enough to keep me going. I finish it faster than I normally drink coffee, and it gives me a slight boost. But deep down, I know I'm fighting a losing battle against exhaustion.

I can't say exactly how many songs have played by now. The music has become a blur in the background as my eyelids grow heavier. The last song I clearly remember hearing is OutKast's "Ms. Jackson." Somewhere in the middle of it, sleep finally catches up with me, and I drift off without even realizing it.

The Sixth Dream

As I begin drifting off into this dream, I'm pleasantly surprised to find myself in a more normal environment. I'm sitting on the back patio of a house I don't recognize. The patio is a comfortable size, furnished with chairs, a grill, and a porch swing. The leaves are turning on the few trees in front of me. There is also a little bit of a chill in the air.

I look around. It looks like I'm in the middle of the country. I see one house ahead of me about a mile away, but it is mainly surrounded by farmland. My focus then returns back to the patio. I look over my shoulder to the right and see a door that leads inside the house. Before I can even get up out of my chair, the door opens. I expect to see Cody, but much to my surprise, someone else comes out of that door. It's Melanie.

"What? How? Am I in one of your dreams?" asks Melanie, who looks as if she's in complete shock.

"You are! Or am I in your dream? Maybe it's your dream. I don't recall the last time I had a dream start off this normally," I say to her.

"Maybe, but the way that I'm engaging with you, and you with me, I feel like this is not an ordinary dream," Melanie says.

"True. I see that you came from the house; how was it inside?" I ask.

"Nothing out of the ordinary. It seemed like a normal house. I don't recognize the house. It's no house I've lived in or been to before. Maybe you should take a look inside and see if you recognize it," says Melanie.

"Sure, I'll take a look around," I respond.

We both step into the house and everything appears normal. It looks like a typical home. The first room we walk into from the patio is the dining room, with a large kitchen situated just to the left.

We make our way to the front of the house. When we get to the front door, there is a huge living room to the right and a hallway that connects to it, leading to what we assume are the bedrooms.

"How much did you explore the house? Also, what part of the house were you in when you entered the dream?" I ask.

"I didn't explore. When I came into the dream, I found myself lying on the couch in the living room. I was planning to look around some, but then I saw you sitting on the back patio. I didn't know it was you until you turned around to look at me," says Melanie.

"Ah, I see. So as far as we know, there's no one else here," I say.

"Yes. However, I have a gut feeling that there's someone or something in one of those rooms," says Melanie.

I do think that Melanie's feeling is right. This house seems too empty and too quiet. I feel as if something is going to happen at any point. As we enter the hallway, there are five doors: two doors on the left, two on the right, and one at the end of the hallway, straight ahead.

"So, Doctor, do you want to check the rooms together? I'm not comfortable with us splitting up."

"Don't worry, Melanie. We'll just check them one at a time together."

We start with the door closest to us, which is the first door on the left. We both take a deep breath, then slowly open the door. The room is a regular-sized bedroom. There is a bunk bed and toys everywhere. This is definitely a kid's room. We notice that the toys don't look like the ones Melanie and I grew up with. They look like newer generation toys such as Game Boy Advances and Bratz dolls.

We leave that room and go across the hallway to the first room on the right. It's simply a bathroom. We cross the hallway again to the second door on the left. We open the door. It looks like a spare room. There is nothing inside. We think it's odd that there is absolutely nothing in there, not even junk.

We then go to the second room on the right, open it, and see that it is another spare room.

"This is weird," says Melanie. "I've never been in a house with two completely empty spare rooms before."

We have one room left to check. Melanie and I look at each other, wondering if what we are supposed to find is behind that door. Maybe we have watched too many movies, but it seems logical that whatever we are looking for might be in the last room. We take a deep breath and open the door, not knowing what to expect on the other side. The door opens to what we assume is the master bedroom. There is a huge California king bed in the middle and a ceiling fan above.

Nothing appears unusual. We are not sure what we are supposed to find, but we expect some kind of clue, maybe a disruption or an odd presence, anything that could give us direction. Up to this point, the dream feels meaningless.

"Unless there is something in the kitchen or dining room. This dream is turning out to be a dud," I say.

"Sure is," Melanie replies.

We turn around and start heading down the hallway.

"Do you think we'll find a chest here?" Melanie asks.

"Not sure. If we will, it might be in some of the more hidden places of the house. Like the basement or..."

"The attic. That's always a good place to look."

Melanie and I scream. We turn around and see Cody.

"Cody! How did you end up in here?" Melanie asks.

"Let's not worry about me. Come with me quickly. I'll take you both to the chest," Cody says.

He suddenly takes off down the hallway, moving fast and with purpose. Melanie and I don't hesitate. We rush after him, our footsteps echoing through the quiet house. He goes into the master bedroom and tells one of us to pull down the stairs to get to the attic. I reach up and pull the string to lower the stairs. Cody goes up first and then we follow. As we enter the attic, we notice that there is not much space up here. It feels very claustrophobic. That feeling fades after we see the chest sitting there in the corner. I reach into my pocket and pull out the key. I quickly insert the key into the next keyhole, the one with the horse's head above it. As usual, I hear the sound of locks moving and clicking inside. Once the sound stops, Cody disappears right in front of us.

"What happens now?" Melanie asks.

"If this goes the way it usually does in my previous dreams, we should be coming into a memory of Cody's," I respond.

I keep waiting for some indication that we are about to be in a memory, but there is nothing.

"Did something go wrong?" Melanie asks.

"I don't know."

Right after I speak, I hear a loud, booming voice come from the bedroom below.

"Who left the attic door open again?" says a man we do not recognize. He has messy dark brown hair, is on the taller side, and has a bit of a beer belly. He is white but very tan.

That is when it occurs to me. Maybe everything we are supposed to discover is inside this house. I tell Melanie that the people in his memories usually cannot see us, so we should head downstairs to find out what is happening. We make our way down and into the hallway. That is when we hear a little girl crying in the kids' bedroom we saw earlier. We hurry to the room just as a man and woman rush right through us and enter.

"Is it Cody again?" the woman asks.

The little girl is sniffling, tears streaming down her face. "No," she responds, but there is some hesitancy in her voice.

"Little girl, I'm getting sick of you lying for him. Now, I will ask you again. Did Cody do it again?" the woman asks.

I don't know who these people are, but I assume they must be Cody's parents. Either way, the woman looks furious, and she is frightening me.

"Yes, Mom. It was him. But please, don't hurt him this time," cries the little girl, who I assume is Cody's sister.

The mom pushes Cody's sister aside as she and the dad rush toward Cody, who is standing in the hallway. They get right in his face, shouting at him.

"Why do you keep doing this to your sister?"

"You are nothing but a freak."

"I can't wait until you're gone."

Both Melanie and I grow angrier the longer we have to listen to this. It looks as if they are about to strike Cody, but all of a sudden, they both drop to their knees and start to scream. Melanie and I look at each other with confusion, wondering what is going on.

"Why are they screaming? Could Cody be infiltrating their minds?" Melanie asks.

"He very well could be," I respond.

Before we can see what happens next, a bright light flashes out of nowhere. When the light fades, we find ourselves standing on the back patio of the house. We are not sure why we are back here. However, I start to look around and notice that the leaves on the trees are green.

"Did you notice that we're in a different season than when we first got here?" I ask Melanie.

"I did. Only problem is, I have no clue if we went forward in time or backwards," Melanie says.

"Let's go inside and find out."

We enter the house, and nothing seems to have changed, at least at first glance. We go to the living room and see Cody and his sister sitting on the couch while two people we don't recognize sit on the other. We wonder who they are, but it doesn't take long to find out.

"Aunt Mary, can I have chocolate milk?" Cody's sister asks.

"Of course you can, Ashley," the aunt replies.

Ashley. Hearing her name again brings everything rushing back. I remember those rushed therapy sessions and the pressure to get through each one like we were racing against some invisible clock. She carried so much weight for someone her age. A stressed little girl doing her best to protect her brother while barely holding herself together.

Ashley goes into the kitchen to fix herself a glass of chocolate milk when there's loud knocking at the door. Mary gets up and answers it. It's Children's Services. My heart begins to sink because I know I'm the reason this is happening. I don't want to watch, but I know I need to.

"We are here to remove the children from this home," one of the social workers says.

"I know what that psychiatrist said about Cody, but are you seriously just going to take her word on this? Yes, I've had my suspicions, but the more I'm around him, the less I see him being able to do what she's accusing him of! Also, why are you taking them both out of our home?" Mary asks.

"While the concern is around Cody, we are concerned that Ashley may be triggered if she stays in this house," the other social worker says.

Mary and her husband Gerald argue with the social workers, but it's no use. Both Cody and Ashley are removed from the home. They kick and scream, not wanting to leave. After they're placed in the car, one of the social workers comes up to Mary and Gerald and gives them a brief overview of the plan. They are open to working toward reuniting Ashley with Mary and Gerald, but reunification with Cody isn't even being considered. Mary is devastated. It's a painful mix of grief and frustration.

"No! I made a promise to my sister that I would watch over her kids!" Mary cries.

Promise? What happened to her sister and her husband? I'd wondered where they were after seeing Mary and Gerald, but I just figured they were babysitting. I didn't realize they actually had some form of custody over the kids. Children's Services withheld a fair amount of information from me when they referred Ashley. The more I think about it, the more it hits me just how rushed everything was to get Ashley out of that home.

I hope to learn more, especially with the sudden time jump and no explanation of what happens in between. But unfortunately, Melanie and I wake up at the same time, which brings the dream to an end.

When we both wake up, we look at each other, clearly distraught over what we just witnessed. One of the flight attendants makes an announcement that we're beginning our descent into

Denver. I'm so relieved that we will soon be getting off this flight. I'm very nervous about what we are going to find in Torrington. It feels like this entire situation keeps taking a darker turn every chance it gets.

There's one thing I don't understand though. The last two times I opened a section of the chest, I understood why I was shown the memory. This time, it feels like I only get fragments of what took place. I really hope I can find more information at Gary's apartment. I hope he has the answers we need, because that dream has left me with more questions than ever.

Chapter 16

Coming Together Slowly

We eventually land in Denver. We both need to use the bathroom, but I let Melanie go first while I watch our carry-ons. While she is in the bathroom, I look at the flight information display. What catches my eye are the canceled flights for Richmond, both Washington airports, and Philadelphia. I'm not sure what to make of all that, other than the fact that it must be related to Salus. That is not our immediate concern right now. Right now, we need to focus on finding out where Gary lives and hopefully find the last pieces of this very confusing puzzle.

Melanie finishes, so I go ahead and head to the bathroom. Afterwards, we make our way to the rental car section of the airport. We just need something decent on gas, so we get a Toyota Corolla. We make our way to the car and start discussing what we are going to do.

"I made arrangements to stay at a hotel I used to work at in Torrington called King's Inn. It's a decent little hotel. Not the fanciest place in the world but not the worst. I figure we can stop to get dinner on the way, then go straight to the hotel. My friend Juliet is still waiting to hear back from a few people, and she'll let us know in the morning what she found out," says Melanie.

"Okay, nice. How long's the drive?" I ask.

"Just under three hours," Melanie says with a shrug. "Out here, that's nothing."

I give her a look. "Says the girl who makes playlists for a trip to the grocery store."

She smirks. "Exactly. I'm prepared."

We both laugh as we start to make our way to I-25, heading north to Wyoming. The scenery is absolutely stunning. Being this close to the Rocky Mountains is surreal; it feels like they stretch endlessly into the sky. Back when I lived in Kansas, I had always planned to visit Colorado but never made it that far west. I cannot help feeling a little envious of Melanie; she has lived all over the western United States, surrounded by landscapes like this. It is such a striking contrast to life back east.

Despite having that stressful dream on the plane, I'm surprised that I feel so rested. I usually don't after these dreams, which I am thankful for, because I really do not want to fall asleep tonight. I'm not sure if I can take two dreams in one day like this. We stop to get chicken fingers and continue making our way to Wyoming. Melanie goes on to talk some more about her time in Torrington. We discover that we both were somewhat loners in high school. We talk about the irony of being friends with a few other loners yet that title still stuck. We share some laughs as we talk about our respective towns of Torrington and Douglasville. Then we decide to do some car karaoke because even though we are well rested, long car trips do tend to make us a bit sleepy.

We fill the time with music, everything from hip hop to country to rock, but there's an odd weight to the air, like the laughter is covering something up. It is strange how time slips away when you're trying to hold on to normalcy. Before I know it, we are pulling into Torrington, and the fun we have been having feels distant, almost like a distraction from whatever is waiting for us there.

We drive into town from the south. I start seeing some buildings somewhat sporadically spread out until we get closer to the center of town. Before we get to town, we make a right turn into King's Inn. We get checked in and make our way into our room. Melanie just gets us a standard room with two queen-size beds.

As we start getting situated for the night, I open up the laptop to see if Director Lynne has contacted me back. Much to my surprise, she has not. I'm really starting to get worried. She has not even read what I sent. So, I decide to try again.

Dr_Kor: Director, are you there? Is there a reason you have not read what I've recently sent you?

Still nothing. I don't know what to make of this. I just hope it's nothing sinister and that maybe it's just a connection issue. I close the laptop and go ahead and brush my teeth for the night. I still don't plan on going to sleep though.

"Are you going to try and get some sleep, Melanie?"

"I don't know. That dream was really freaky. I've never experienced something like that in my life. I know I asked if it was possible that you and I could be in the same dream together, but I didn't think that it was actually going to happen."

"Neither did I, Melanie. So, what's the plan tomorrow?"

168

"Juliet is going to come by at seven tomorrow morning. She is going to inform us of what she was able to find out. She is hoping to narrow down the leads by morning," says Melanie.

"I hope she'll have something by then," I say to Melanie.

I get on the burner phone and start scrolling through news stories to see if anything else unusual is happening when I suddenly receive a notification from Snapchat. It catches me off guard. I hardly ever use Snapchat, but I installed it on this phone because some of my students back in Oxford prefer to contact me that way. A few of them hate using email, so I wanted to make sure I stayed accessible to them. Still, the real surprise is not the notification itself. It is who the snap is from. It is from Lauren.

"Melanie, look at this."

"What is going on?"

"I received a snap from Lauren," I respond.

We both sit up in our respective beds and move toward the middle, facing each other. I open the snap, and it's a picture of Gary tied up. The caption on the snap reads:

It'll be too late by the time you find everything.

"This isn't good! Do you think we can still save Gary?" Melanie asks, her voice tight with worry. "I knew she had taken him, but I was hoping she wouldn't go as far as to endanger his life."

"I'm going to be honest with you," I say quietly. "I don't know. Something about this feels off. I just have a bad feeling we might be too late. I really hope I'm wrong."

I don't know how to respond to Lauren. I fear that any response I give might shorten the time we have to try to save Gary's life. So, I don't want to push anything. I even consider blocking her. However, maybe she will slip up if she continues to send snaps, and that might give us some of the information we desperately need.

We both drop back onto our beds, eyes locked on the TV like it can somehow drown out what we have just seen in Lauren's snap. The image of Gary sticks with me. It is unsettling, urgent, and completely out of reach. He is in danger. He needs our help. We need to do something. We have to find a way to help him. But what can we even do from here? We have no plan, no lead, and no idea where he really is.

The helplessness troubles me, but so does the exhaustion. A slow, heavy wave of exhaustion is already pulling me down. I don't want to fall asleep. Not when someone's life could be in danger. Not when every time I close my eyes, I risk being pulled into something else I still don't understand. I look over at Melanie. She looks just as torn. Her eyes are heavy, but I can see the tension in her face like she is trying to resist what her body has already decided. We're both worn down, but neither of us wants to give in.

We should be figuring this out. We should be trying harder. Doing something. Anything.

"You need sleep," I tell myself.

If I'm going to help him, I need my strength.

I'm not sure I truly believe it. It feels like something I'm telling myself just to cope. But right now, it's all I've got. If I don't hold on to something, even if it's fragile, I'll fall apart. So, I close my eyes, push the fear aside, and try to let my strength return.

The alarm on my phone blares and wakes me up. It is 6:15 AM. I start to go back to sleep, but then I shoot up out of bed. Wait a minute. Did I really fall asleep and not have a dream? Finally!

It's about time. I'm so excited. Then a thought crosses my mind. Is this temporary? I'm not sure, but either way, the excitement fades quickly. I decide to stay up for the rest of the day.

I grab my phone to check for any updates on Gary. I'm seriously worried about him. Guilt keeps creeping in. I slept instead of trying harder to figure out what is going on. I keep telling myself I was exhausted and needed the rest, but that does not stop the guilt from eating at me. I decide to send Lauren a message asking for an update on Gary. I sit on the bed for twenty minutes, waiting for her to read it and respond. Nothing. I keep wondering why she chose to contact me through Snapchat in the first place.

I desperately want to hear back from Lauren, so while I wait, I decide to go get coffee. I go to Melanie's nightstand, grab the keys to the rental car and the DHS credit card, and head out. I just want to find a convenience store. I don't know this town, but I remember Melanie talking a lot about a place called Smoker Friendly. That is where I end up going. I get the coffee and return to the hotel room. We both finish getting ready for the day and sit down at the table, drinking our coffee.

"Any word from Lauren about Gary?" Melanie asks.

"Nothing yet," I reply. "I sent her a message this morning asking for an update on his condition and if there's any way we can help secure his release. So far, I have not heard back."

Melanie stares at the wall, her eyes beginning to fill with tears. She finally speaks, her voice soft. "Gary put himself in a really difficult position by coming to us and sharing what he knew. I'd hate to think that we might end up being the reason something happens to him."

"Melanie, we cannot force people to do anything. We all have free will. If she chooses to do something to him, that's on her, not on us," I say.

We sit in silence, neither of us knowing what's going to happen to Gary. After a few minutes, I decide to break the silence by talking about how my sleep went.

"Guess what? I did not have a dream at all last night. It felt nice actually getting some sleep and not waking up stressed," I say.

"Nice. I'm glad that you caught a break. I did dream, but it was a normal dream," Melanie replies.

The time is 6:50 AM. I listen to Melanie tell me about her dream. She's working as a photographer in Iceland, married with kids. She's not sure why she dreamed it. She never even considered living in Iceland. While she is talking, there is a knock at the door. Melanie gets up, looks through the peephole, and sees that it is Juliet. She opens the door and the two of them hug each other for a good bit.

"Juliet, allow me to introduce you to Dr. Geneva Koraline," says Melanie.

"Pleasure to meet you, Juliet," I say.

"Pleasure is mine, Dr. Koraline," says Juliet.

The three of us sit at the table. Juliet pulls out some papers and starts to discuss her findings.

"Okay, here is the deal. We have 20 tenants named Gary in this town. That's when I decided to switch up my tactics. I started looking at people who moved here around the time that Melanie told me he came to Torrington. That narrowed it down to four possibilities and I was going to discuss with you how we would check on all four properties. However, an hour ago, a landlord that

I'm friends with said that he has something weird going on at one of his apartments," says Juliet.

"What is going on?" I ask.

"He says it's hard to explain, but there was some black and purple glow very lightly coming from the apartment. He wasn't sure what to do, but I told him I would talk to the two of you first. I don't know why you need to find Gary, but the fact that Melanie said she really could not tell me much made me wonder if there was a connection," says Juliet.

"That apartment might be exactly what we're looking for. The black and purple glow matches what we're looking for. There has to be some kind of connection. How soon can we get over there?" Melanie asks.

"I'll shoot him a text and find out if he's available anytime soon," says Juliet. In the meantime, you two can follow me to the property. Even if he is not there yet, you can still get a general look around before he arrives."

Sounds like a good plan. Let's head out," I respond.

While we are getting ready to leave the room, I hear a faint couple of pings on my side of the bed. It's my laptop. I'm surprised they don't hear it. Maybe Director Lynne has finally messaged me back. I get up from the table and go to retrieve the laptop.

"The two of you go ahead and get the cars started, I have to go to the bathroom," I say to them, hoping they'll believe the lie. I don't need Juliet being involved in this any further.

They leave the room, and as soon as the door closes, I grab the laptop.

I see that I do have a message from Director Lynne.

Dir_Lynne: Sorry for the delayed response. We've been dealing with a massive situation here. We've lost all contact with Oxford. The issue started at the University of Oxford but then it spread to the entire city. It has been engulfed in a strange black and purple veil. Do you have any idea what's going on?

Dr_Kor: There's a huge chance that the veil is connected to the mysterious being Salus. Though I'm concerned that stuff is happening all the way over there. He keeps growing in power!

Dir_Lynne: I hope that all of you are able to find a solution to this. By the way, to answer your question, we did try to trace Gary's IP address, but we have failed.

Dr_Kor: Ok, well thanks anyway. Though, we have a lead now that looks like it could be our smoking gun for what we're looking for.

Dir_Lynne: That's good. If anything else comes up, I'll try to let you know. However, I won't be in contact very much due to the ongoing crisis here at home.

Dr_Kor: I understand. The same will be true on my end. Be careful and good luck.

Dir_Lynne: You too.

Chat ended.

I walk outside to where Juliet and Melanie are waiting.

"Good news. He says that the two of you can visit the property. He will unlock the apartment, but he says he will not stick around. He really is freaked out about what's going on there."

"That was fast. I guess you do not need to take us there, huh?" Melanie says.

"Nope. You can find the place with your phone. I'll text the address," Juliet says.

"Thank you, Juliet. We really appreciate your help," Melanie says.

"No problem. I don't know what this is all about, but the two of you, please promise me you'll be careful," Juliet says.

"We'll try our hardest," I say.

Melanie and Juliet hug before Juliet goes on her way. We soon get into the rental car and prepare ourselves to investigate Gary's apartment. After Melanie enters the address into the phone, it looks like the apartments are located just a little north of town. They are about five minutes from the town center.

I stare out the window, then turn to Melanie. "This all feels a little too easy. Your friend happens to have the information we need and gets Gary's address, and suddenly we are closing in on where Gary lives? Something about it does not sit right with me."

Melanie nods slowly and says, "I've been thinking the same thing. It's moving a little too perfectly, like someone wants us to find out what he has been up to."

"What if it's a setup? What if we're walking straight into a trap?"

"Then we walk in smart. We stay alert, but we keep moving. If Gary is in danger, we do not have time to second guess every lead."

I respond with a hesitant nod.

"Agreed. We just need to be careful. If this is a trap, we cannot afford to spring it blindly" I say hesitantly.

We head up and I'm a bit surprised by what we find. The apartment complex used to be a motel, and I don't think I've ever seen one converted like that before. We drive in slowly, our eyes scanning the parking lot. There are no other cars. We cannot tell if everyone is away at work or if Gary is the only person living here. Either possibility is unsettling.

The stillness around the complex makes the tension even heavier. The place feels deserted, like time has stopped. We park a few spots away from his apartment, not wanting to risk anything happening to the car with how uncertain things have become. As we approach the door, the black and purple veil vanishes entirely. We are not sure what to make of it, but we know we have to keep going. I open the door, and as we step inside, we find ourselves in the living room. The space is in complete disarray. Papers are scattered everywhere, covering nearly every surface.

"Oh great… Where do we even start?" Melanie asks.

"I don't know. The best option right now is just to pick a pile and start going through it," I reply.

"Sounds like a plan. We also need to keep an eye out for anything that could help us figure out where Lauren could be taking Gary," Melanie says.

She's right. Every second counts.

Melanie stays in the living room while I venture further into the apartment to find the bedroom and look in there. His bedroom is not much better. Papers are scattered everywhere in there too. I decide to start with the ones on his bed, though I'm not exactly looking forward to it. Messes like this stress me out, and it doesn't help that it is not even my mess. The worst part is, I have no clue what I'm supposed to be looking for, and time is slipping away.

Melanie and I go through countless piles of papers. They look like research papers and analysis of what they did in Socorro. I'm not really finding anything that would help us out. After about an hour, I decide to send Lauren a message asking about Gary. I tell her I need proof that he's still alive. A few minutes later, she responds with a Snap. It is a blurry photo of Gary, still tied up, looking dazed. The caption reads:

Time is running out.

My chest tightens. That is not what I need. I want answers. Where is she taking him? What is she planning to do? I send another message, trying to keep calm.

"What do you want from us? Is there anything we can do to help get him released?"

A minute passes. Then two.

Finally, she responds, "You want him back? Then I need something from you. Both of you."

That is it. No details. No demands. Just more questions piling on top of the ones I already have. I'm getting tired of the cryptic messages and the power games. I message again.

"What do you need? We're willing to listen. Just tell us what you want."

No answer.

I stare at the screen, waiting for the indication that she is typing. Nothing.

I look over at Melanie.

"We need to figure this out fast," I say. "Because whatever game Lauren is playing, Gary is running out of time."

Two more hours pass as we look through countless piles of papers. We're just at a loss trying to find something that we don't know. We're both about to stop to take a break until Melanie yells,

"I THINK I FOUND SOMETHING!"

I rush into the living room and Melanie is standing there with a digital voice recorder in hand.

"I found this voice recorder. The word 'investigation' is written with a sharpie on the back. That really piqued my interest," says Melanie.

"I'm sure it has to have something we need. Let's make space on this couch and listen to it," I say to Melanie.

We clear off space on the couch and sit down. Melanie looks at the available recordings and sees that there's only one file on there. We are not sure if there were others and they got deleted, or if he just started using this one. There is only one way to find out. Melanie presses play and turns the volume all the way up.

This is the last recording that I'm going to do. I'm losing my mind here trying to understand what goes down in New Mexico. I put the blame for what is happening on all of us who are involved. I just figure that perhaps this is some type of punishment for how Cody is treated during the last few months before the incident at the facility. However, there's one thing that's really weird to me. It's with Lauren. I didn't think much about it at first, but I cannot shake this feeling that something more must've happened when Lauren took Cody past the VLA. I feel guilty for placing additional blame on her. Still, it's very strange to me that she would warn me not to come back to the facility, despite not thinking she is involved, I need to do some research on her. I have to. Everything points back to that day she has Cody and takes that unauthorized trip with him. Fortunately, I'm able to form a friendship with a few people here in town. They have a decent number of connections and resources to help find information for me. I do what I can to find out about Lauren and her past. However, I make a startling discovery. The name that she uses, Lauren Appleton, is not her actual identity. There are no records of this person existing until a year after the project gets underway. I contact the state she claims she is from. She says she is originally from New York. There are no records in New York that match the information she gives me. I have no idea where she is originally from. So, I'm pretty much back to square one. I feel like I am going in circles. She has no social media pages. The only picture I have of her is one she gives me of her and her cousin. Her cousin is in the army. She claims he's in the New York National Guard and has been in the National Guard his entire career. She also says that he lives about two hours from her. I'm stuck. I don't know what else to do."

Listening to that recording makes me question Gary and numerous things he tells me back in Virginia. Why didn't he tell me this face to face? Maybe he wasn't completely sure he can trust me.

"That's it. There's nothing else on here," says Melanie.

"I wish we had more clues. Maybe we can at least look at the picture if we can find it," I say to Melanie.

"I did see that picture earlier. However, I wasn't sure what I was looking at, so I just placed it in one of the piles," Melanie says.

"Do you remember which pile?" I ask.

"Yeah, one of these two piles on the right side of the couch," she responds.

We both take a pile and start going through it. I do eventually find the picture. Lauren is standing next to her cousin, who is wearing an army uniform with a large black number 1 patch on his left sleeve. We finally get a clear view of what Lauren looks like. I'd seen her before in previous dreams, but she was partially hidden, her features obscured. Now, seeing her fully, I see her brunette hair, average height, and a beautiful, warm smile. There's something about her that feels oddly familiar, though I can't quite place why.

"I feel like I might have seen her before," I say.

"What a crazy day. To come all the way out here and justify what, a picture?" Melanie says frustratingly.

"It is very frustrating," says Melanie.

"Let's send this picture to Carly and Matthew. Maybe they can make some sense of it," I suggest.

Melanie grabs the phone, snaps a picture, and sends it in a group text to Matthew and Carly. She also texts a description of the photo and explains how we come across it in the first place. The picture is taken at such an angle that we cannot even make out the last name on the uniform.

Five minutes after Melanie sends off the group text, Matthew calls Melanie's phone. Melanie answers and then puts the phone on speaker.

"Hello?"

"Yes, Melanie, is Dr. Koraline there with you?" asks Matthew.

"I am," I respond.

"Good. Okay, I got a good look at the picture. There are some discrepancies with what Lauren told Gary based on this picture," says Matthew.

"Oh? What are the issues?" I ask.

"I'm an Army Veteran. I know a decent amount of the more popular patches. There's no way that he's in the New York National Guard, or at least he wasn't when this picture was taken. If you look at his arm, you'll see a patch with the number one in bold in the middle. That patch belongs to the 1st Infantry Division, which is an active-duty unit based out of Fort Riley, Kansas. Now, National Guard units can get activated for active duty, but I don't believe this is the case here. I believe this soldier was stationed in Kansas. Which, if the other parts of the story are true about her cousin only living close to two hours away from her, then it's possible that Lauren may be from Kansas and not New York," says Matthew.

"Huh. That's very interesting. What you're saying is making sense," I say.

"Thank you for your help, Matthew," Melanie says.

"You're welcome. Keep us posted," Matthew says and he ends the call.

There's an open water bottle near Melanie, and she accidentally bumps into it. Water spills onto the picture.

"Oh no! I didn't mean for that to happen! I'm so sorry!" Melanie exclaims.

"It's okay. We have a copy of it anyway. We are good. I'll go grab some paper towels from the kitchen," I say.

I start to grab some paper, but Melanie's frantic voice suddenly calls out to me.

"Dr. Koraline! The water, it reveals something on the back of this photo!"

I run back in to find Melanie standing there, her mouth open in shock, clearly surprised by something she has just discovered. I run over to her and take the photo from her.

"Looks like whoever made this wanted the message hidden until just the right moment," I say. "Some inks react to moisture. It's an old trick, but effective."

I stare as faint letters begin to emerge on the paper, gradually becoming clear. Wait… no. That cannot be right.

We found this pic when we were doing spring cleaning. Figured you'd want it. Love you, Ashley!

Aunt Mary

I read the message aloud so Melanie can hear it clearly. We lock eyes, both stunned as the truth sinks in. Lauren, the one who has been working against us and secretly helping Salus... is Ashley. Cody's sister!

Chapter 17

Back to the Beginning

I'm in a complete state of shock. I can't believe that this whole time, Lauren is actually Cody's sister. Now that we know her real name, I guess we can start referring to her as Ashley. I've been wondering why she looked vaguely familiar to me. I haven't seen Ashley since she was a kid, but some of her facial features remind me of someone I might've met before. This revelation clears up a few things, but it also opens the door to even more questions. Why would Ashley align herself with Salus? It makes sense that she might join the project to keep an eye on her brother, but what I can't wrap my head around is why she would choose to work alongside a being like that.

"Do you think this may be what Gary wanted us to find?" Melanie asks.

"While this is an important discovery, I don't think Gary knew about it. I think what he was intending for us to find is still in here somewhere," I respond.

We continue digging through papers when an idea comes to me.

"Melanie, we now know that Lauren is actually Ashley, but there's still one thing we don't know much about," I say.

"What?" she responds.

"His childhood. His life with his biological parents. While we're here, we should see if there's anything we can find out about Cody. Maybe that's what Gary is trying to lead us to," I say.

"That would make sense. I think there's a file cabinet in the corner. We can start going through it," Melanie says.

We go over to the file cabinet and start looking through it. It doesn't take us long to find what we're looking for. I come across a folder that has the logo of the Kansas Department of Children and Families. Melanie and I return to the couch and start going through the folder.

There isn't much information. How did he even get access to this in the first place? The earliest file we find is dated July 30, 2013. We're not sure exactly what the document is, but we read the case worker's notes:

Cody won't tell us anything. He swears that he isn't doing anything. I want to believe him, I really do. However, this situation is too weird. It doesn't make any sense. I'm not sure what we can do for him. I'm not sure if we have enough to admit him to psychiatric. However, maybe a break from that house wouldn't be a bad thing. He has been through a lot in that house. I definitely think some time with a foster family would do him some good.

"This tells us a little bit, but it's not really giving us the answers we need," says Melanie.

"I agree. Let's see if there's anything else in this folder that can help us."

We keep going through the rest of the folder and come across several documents. Unfortunately, most of them repeat the same

184

notes we saw in the earliest file. That changes when we reach the final document in the folder.

Maybe the dreams are real. For years, we didn't have any verification. Until yesterday. That was really frightening what took place. Regardless, it's out of our hands now.

"Out of our hands now? This information is so vague. A part of me feels like they might be keeping it vague on purpose," I say to Melanie.

"It does seem that way," Melanie replies as she checks the page for the date. "The date reads Monday, January 13, 2020."

"Three years ago. That would have been around the time Cody ended up under DHS."

"True. I just wish we had more information about what happened during his time in state custody. It's like a lot is being left out of these reports," Melanie says.

"Hold on, we might have something here," I say, pointing to a name on the report. John Robert.

"John Robert? Looks like he was Cody's last foster parent before he was moved to Socorro, if I'm remembering the dates right," Melanie says.

"There's a phone number listed. Let's call him and see what we can find out," I say.

Melanie hands me her phone, and I dial the number. It rings twice before someone picks up.

"Hello?"

"Yes, is this John Robert?"

"Yes, it is. Who am I speaking to?"

"My name is Dr. Koraline. I've recently been assigned to work with a young boy who used to be in your care named Cody," I say.

There is silence. I wait, but he says nothing. After several seconds, I start to wonder if he has hung up. I glance at the screen and see that the call is still connected. I try again.

"Is there anything you can tell us about Cody? We were not given much information," I say to him.

Still no response.

"What can you tell me about his dreams?" I ask.

Nothing. Not even background noise. Melanie motions to me, so I mute the call and turn toward her.

"Maybe he's too afraid to talk on the phone. Should we offer to meet him in Kansas?" she suggests.

"If he still lives in Kansas. It is worth a try," I respond. I unmute the call. "Would you prefer to talk in person?"

I hear faint breathing, then finally a whisper. "Yes. Meet me in Shawnee, Kansas. Text me when you are nearby, and I'll give you more instructions." Then he ends the call.

"Great. Now we wait," I say. "Melanie, your idea worked, but I really hoped he would just talk to us now."

"I hoped so too. I figured he might be scared," Melanie replies.

"Here's the plan. Let's take the file and voice recorder with us, grab our stuff from the hotel, and head back to Denver. While we are driving, we can go ahead and book us a flight from Denver to Kansas City. We need to get there as soon as possible."

"Sounds good. I'll start as soon as we are in the car," Melanie says.

We grab the file and the recorder and head back to the car. We are not sure if we need to leave the apartment door open, so we leave it unlocked. Melanie sends Juliet a text letting her know we are done.

As we pull into the hotel parking lot, Carly calls.

"Hello, Carly," Melanie answers.

"Have either of you been on social media or seen the news lately?" Carly asks.

"No. Why?" I ask.

"The weird black and purple veil has completely engulfed DC. No one is able to get in or out of the city. We're not able to communicate with anybody. Most of the upper echelon of our government is still there. There is a bit of a scramble to try and figure out how to get into the city or who should temporarily run the country. Our entire line of succession is in DC currently. I know there's probably not much you can do about it right now, but I'm just letting you know that you should expect chaos over the course of the day and beyond."

Melanie and I exchange a stunned look, both at a loss for words. Unsure of what else to do, I go ahead and fill Carly in on what we found at Gary's apartment and where we plan to head next.

"Well, I have some bad news for the two of you. I definitely think that it's important to talk to this foster parent, but the FAA is about to ground the majority of air traffic in the country. So, you will have to drive there. I imagine it is not a short drive, but until you or somebody finds some answers on what is going on, it is better to be safe than sorry," says Carly.

187

"Okay, this sucks though. We'll try to get there as quickly and safely as possible. We'll let you or Matthew know when we have arrived in Kansas," says Melanie.

I then decide to update Carly on what Lauren, or rather Ashley, sent through Snapchat along with the latest information we have about Gary.

"That is not good. Did you take screenshots of the snaps?" Carly asks.

"I did," I reply and text them to her.

"There's not much we can do on our end. We'll take the screenshots and see if we can find any clues to Gary's whereabouts," Carly says. "Be safe out there. Good luck."

"Good luck to you too," I say and hang up.

"Do you think DC is being attacked?" asks Melanie.

"I honestly do not know. Salus has not revealed what his plans are. Let's pack up and leave as soon as possible," I suggest.

"Sounds good," replies Melanie.

We rush to the hotel room and gather all our stuff as quickly as possible. It's already 1:30 PM and we have a nine-and-a-half-hour trip to make. What is worse is the fact that we lose an hour somewhere in Nebraska as we cross into central time. Which means if we take into account any breaks that we need to take, it may be around eleven or midnight before we even get into Shawnee. Another long night ahead.

I'm doing everything I can to try to keep an optimistic outlook, but I feel like we simply don't have the time to make this drive. Things seem to be growing worse by the hour, and we need to find all the answers quickly.

We get into the car and drive to the office. I quickly get out to drop off the hotel room keys. As soon as I get back in the car, we start making our way to Kansas. I decide to turn on the radio to see if we can get any more information on what is going on in DC. Let's just say I'm not prepared for the reports that are coming in.

If you're just now tuning in, a monumental crisis is unfolding in our nation right now. We have no way to explain it, and there doesn't seem to be a single expert who can offer a reasonable explanation for what's happening. Everything begins earlier today when the entirety of DC becomes surrounded by a strange black and purple veil or mist. No one knows for sure what it is. We just know that every attempt to enter it has failed. Vehicles trying to drive through crash into it, as if they are slamming into a brick wall. While all of this is happening in DC, we begin receiving unconfirmed reports of black and purple lightning striking in Oxford, over in the United Kingdom. British authorities are baffled by what they are witnessing. Please stay tuned as we work to bring you updates on this developing situation. We ask for your patience as we do our best to verify all information before sharing it. This is Charles Thompson, reporting for Worldwide News Today.

"That's weird. If what's happening in Oxford is really Salus, why is he targeting Oxford? I ask. "I really hope my colleagues and students are okay."

"Do you think he will attack anywhere else?" Melanie asks.

"I'm sure he will. We just need to figure out what his game plan is," I reply.

We listen to the news for about another hour before switching back to music. Since there are no updates, we decide to check the news every hour just in case anything changes. We think about checking social media, but there are not many posts coming out of the affected areas. I do see a lot of people panicking online though and true to our new American tradition since the COVID shutdowns in 2020, everyone is rushing to buy toilet paper again.

I put my phone down and stare out the window for a while. There's not much to see. Just stretches of farmland and open prairie. Sometimes it's beautiful, but other times, it gets boring fast. I decide to close my eyes for a bit since I will be taking over driving halfway through the trip. The scenery is making me extra tired. I'm not sure what is going to happen, but I have a strong feeling another dream is on its way. About ten minutes later, I fall asleep.

I wake up, and to my surprise, I have not dreamed at all.

"How long have I been asleep?" I ask.

"Well, we're almost to the halfway point where you take over, so it's been a few hours at least," Melanie responds.

"I see. Any updates on what's going on?" I ask.

"Mostly the same, except for one major development," she says.

"Oh? What is it?"

"They are in a rush to figure out who will take over leadership of the country for now. Since the Pentagon is located just outside of Washington, it has not been affected by the veil. The Deputy Secretary of Defense is there. There's talk that he might step in as acting president until contact with Washington can be restored," Melanie responds.

We keep driving, but every mile through Nebraska feels like it's dragging us down, as if we are not supposed to leave. I turn on the radio a couple more times hoping for updates. Aside from a quick mention of Douglasville and some strange lightning activity, there's nothing new.

Eventually, we arrive in Shawnee, Kansas around midnight. We're completely exhausted. We need to meet with John Robert soon, but I'm not even sure if he is willing to talk to us this late. We text Carly to let her know we have made it.

We check into a Comfort Inn and Suites and get the same room setup we had last time. As soon as we walk in, I collapse onto the bed from exhaustion. My eyes are heavy, and I struggle to keep them open. I want to text my mom to get an update about Douglasville, but I cannot get in touch with her. I feel nervous for her and for my friends who still live there.

We turn on the TV and learn that the military is now involved. They had a strategy to try to break through the veil, but they discovered some of the munitions they were using actually went through the veil and into the city. Because of that, the military is backing off and working on a new strategy that will not risk harming anyone inside.

My eyes can't take it anymore. I know I'm about to fall asleep. I try to fight it so I can check on my mom again, but I also know I'm no good to anyone if I'm completely drained tomorrow. As I drift off to sleep, I find myself wondering what kind of dream will come to me this time.

Chapter 18

New Discoveries

The Seventh Dream

This dream starts off in a very weird way, which is really saying something considering the other dreams I've had so far. For a moment, I think I'm awake because I'm in my hotel bed. I look to my left and Melanie is still asleep in her bed. I really believe I'm awake until I see a bright light shining through the window. We're on the first floor, so I assume at first that it's a car. However, it seems too bright for headlights, even LEDs.

So, I open the curtain a little bit, and I can't believe what I see. There are sand dunes everywhere. It doesn't look like I'm in the Sahara or the Middle East. The sand has a whiter color. I've never seen dunes like this before. It's at that point I remember the American Embassy staffer Lea, who told me and the other staffer about her dream. I walk outside, and when the door closes behind me, I can no longer see my room or the hotel.

It's freaky how this environment is nearly identical to Lea's dream. The dunes stretch on forever. It's a bit windy though. I also remember how she saw Cody standing on one of the dunes, so I keep my eye out to see if I can find him. I can't remember what color onesie he was wearing, but I figure he'll stick out like a sore thumb in this place anyway. So, I start walking around this massive place, trying to find him. While I walk, I keep hearing a female voice faintly coming from the sky. I can't tell who it is that's speaking. Maybe it's nothing. I don't dwell on it for long because I just want to find Cody.

I continue on for about five minutes when I notice someone in black clothing standing on a dune about two miles away. That has to be Cody! I begin moving toward him, but something feels off. The closer I get to him, the harder it is to run. Running on sand is already hard enough, but this feels like something is weighing me down. Still, I push forward with all my strength to reach him.

I'm about a quarter of a mile from him when I feel tremendous shaking under the ground. It's the most intense shaking I've ever experienced. I don't have anything to hold onto, so I just sit on the ground and try to wait it out. I keep expecting Salus to appear at any moment, so I prepare myself for the worst. I don't have any weapons on me, nor is anyone around besides Cody. This dream would've been the perfect one for Melanie to be in with me.

The ground eventually stops shaking, and I see the sand shifting in large, rolling waves in front of me. I expect the menacing Salus to appear, but I'm in for a huge shock. It's not him. It's Ashley! She looks like she did in that picture: black hair, pale skin, average height, and gray eyes. Ashley isn't huge or intimidating like Salus, but the way she crosses her arms and narrows her eyes makes it clear she's not in the best mood.

"You have some nerve showing up here," says Ashley.

"What? Do you think I go searching for these dreams? I don't have control over what dreams I have. I still don't understand how any of this is even possible. I'm just trying to restore the natural balance of things here," I reply.

Ashley laughs. Then she's caught in a serious fit of laughter. It's almost like she's going insane.

"Dr. Geneva Koraline! That's hilarious coming out of your mouth. You're the one who created all this in the first place!" says Ashley.

Butterflies churn in my stomach and I feel my pulse racing.

"What do you mean I created all of this?" I ask.

Ashley paces around for a little bit. It seems she's frustrated that I don't understand what she means.

"Okay, 'doctor,' I guess you're not as smart as I thought. Don't you get it? You were supposed to pay attention to what he dreamt about, what I dreamt about. But you wouldn't even give us a chance. You refused to see my brother, not that it would've mattered anyway. You wouldn't listen to me when I tried to talk about my dreams. Sure, you heard me, but you'd already decided that everything I said was just some kind of repressed trauma from my brother. He did absolutely nothing to me, and yet you were so determined to turn him into the villain. How dare you?" Ashley says.

I usually don't cry, especially in front of other people. However, I can't help it. I'm in tears. I don't know if Ashley is telling me the full truth, that I'm the one who created all this. However, there is one thing I do know: I definitely assisted.

"Ashley. I'm sorry. I'm deeply sorry. I was young and right out of school back then. I made numerous mistakes when I first started. I still make mistakes now, but the biggest regret I have is assisting in sending your brother into state custody," I say to Ashley.

"Before or after you got involved?" Ashley asks. I think she is referring to when I found out that her brother was innocent. Was I sorry before or after finding this out?

The truth is, it's after. But saying that out loud could push her over the edge. Based on what I have seen her do while helping Salus, I'm not sure what she might be capable of if I give the wrong answer. Still, I know better than to lie. She would see right through it.

So, I say nothing.

"Maybe you didn't hear me," she says, her voice colder this time. "Were you sorry before or after you got involved?"

I stay quiet, holding my ground. I'm not sure if that is the right call. But I figure if I deny her what she wants, maybe she will slip, say something or make a move I can use. It's risky, but this whole thing has been risky from the start. As we continue this standoff, I can visibly see her getting angrier by the minute. She continues to ask me, each time more aggressive than the last.

She finally stops. She closes her eyes and takes some deep breaths. I'm a bit shocked that she's trying to calm herself down. I take it as a good sign. However, I soon realize how naive I am. She slowly opens her eyes, and she has an evil smile on her face.

"Okay, you do not have to answer me. But you will answer him."

The ground shakes violently again, but this time Salus comes out of the ground. He's not in a human form by any means. He takes the shape of one of the most terrifying creatures I've ever seen in my life. His whole body is just a black void. His red eyes are scarier than previous times I've encountered him. His teeth seem sharper, and the face he makes when he does a deep growl is enough to give me nightmares for weeks. I start backing up some, and out of the blue, Cody is right behind me. I didn't even see him. I back into him on accident.

"Cody, I am sorry for backing into you. I'm also so sorry for how everything turned out in your life," I say through tears.

"Dr. Koraline, it is true that you didn't help," Cody says, "but I think I still would have ended up on this path sooner or later. Here, take this."

He reaches into his pocket and pulls out an antique key. The handle is shaped like a pocket watch, the kind with exposed gears you can see turning inside.

"I really hope the dream with the chest turns out better than this one," I say to him.

"The chest is not in a dream this time," says Cody.

"Not in a dream? So, somewhere in our world?" I ask.

"Yes. The great thing is, you're so close to it already. If you go towards—"

Before he can finish, Salus sends both of us flying. The impact hits like a truck. My body slams against the ground, and pain shoots through my side as I try to catch my breath. I force myself to sit up, but before I can fully stand, Salus grabs me.

His hand clamps around my body like iron, and I wince as pain shoots through me. He yanks me off the ground and pulls me in close until we are face to face. His skin is black as night, like shadow made solid, and his eyes, those burning red eyes, lock onto mine without a single blink. His breath is hot and sharp, like scorched metal, and the sheer size of him makes me feel small, completely powerless in his grip. He stares at me in silence, as if deciding what to do next.

Then finally, he speaks. "I think you've interfered enough. It's time to end this."

His other hand opens up, and I can see the black and purple veil getting ready to come toward me. I'm terrified. I really think this is going to be the end. But I look down toward Cody, and he has his hands extended. A bright light fills the area. It's bright enough to blind Salus, which causes him to drop me. I fall for a long period of time, and right when I'm about to hit the ground, I wake up.

I jolt up in my bed. I'm hyperventilating again. After I calm myself down a little, I notice I have something in my right hand. It's the key Cody gave me. I wish I were able to find where this chest is. I feel like the most important piece to this puzzle is located there. Though I struggle to understand how this chest can exist both in our dreams and here in person, I'm quickly learning that I need to throw logic and reason out the window. This is something else entirely, and I just need to find the answer to stop all of this.

I check my phone and see that it is 6:30 in the morning. I go ahead and get up for the day. After I finish my morning routine, I get out the laptop to see if I missed any messages. I don't see anything. Melanie gets up thirty minutes later. She asks if I had any dreams. I tell her about the dream and do my best not to leave out any details. Afterwards, Melanie looks like she's in shock.

Though she's clearly stunned, I notice her eyes shift with focus. She's already thinking it through, piecing something together. Which I'm glad about, because I need someone with a clear head to see things I might've missed.

"What if Ashley is involved more than we initially realized? When you mentioned that she was contacting Salus in New Mexico, I think we both assumed that he made contact with her first. What if it's the other way around? What if she made first contact with him?" says Melanie.

That is a really good point she brings up. In the dream, it does feel like Ashley is the one who is in control. Then, while we're thinking about that, another big question comes to my mind.

"Melanie, I think you really might be onto something. Because there's something I didn't even think about until you mentioned Ashley being the one to orchestrate this. When I saw Ashley as a child, she was eight years old. With ten years having passed, that makes her eighteen now. How was she able to work on this project as an aide? I understand that aides weren't required to have the same education and qualifications as the rest of us, but I still can't imagine them allowing someone as young as eighteen to be part of this project. She doesn't look eighteen to me, so perhaps that played a role, but the question must still be asked... how?" I tell Melanie, still trying to make sense of everything.

"That's a fair point. Maybe we can find that answer out today," says Melanie.

Melanie finishes getting ready for the day and sends John a text asking where to meet. He replies that we can meet at his house, but not for an extended period of time.

"Is he concerned that he's being monitored?" Melanie asks.

"Probably," I say. "It makes sense. He was Cody's last foster parent before DHS got involved. He might want to help, but keeping the visit short gives him some distance. If anyone starts asking questions, he can say we didn't stay long."

I tell Melanie I'll head to the lobby and grab us breakfast to go. I meet her at the car, and we drive to John Robert's house. It isn't far from the hotel, so we get there in no time.

When we arrive, we catch a glimpse of him peeking through the blinds, making sure it's really us. We had sent him a couple of selfies before leaving the hotel, so he should recognize us. We knock on the door, and I introduce myself as Dr. Koraline, with my assistant Melanie Moon. He cautiously opens the door and tells us to come in quickly.

We follow him into the living room, sit down, and he begins to talk.

"Listen, I'll answer the questions you have for me as best I can, but I want to emphasize that I don't want you both here for very long," John says.

"We understand. We'll get right to it," I reply. "The file we looked at says you were Cody's last foster parent. What happened when he lived in your home?"

"I wasn't fostering alone. My ex-wife was still in my life back then, and we had our two boys. I was skeptical about having Cody in our house after reading the reports from previous foster homes and how he initially ended up in care. But my wife insisted she could help him since she was a psychiatrist. So, we agreed.

"The first couple of months were fine. Nothing seemed out of the ordinary, and we thought maybe the records were exaggerated. But then our boys started complaining about dreams and nightmares that 'Cody would give them.' We tried to get them to explain. They couldn't. They just said Cody would tell them what they'd dream that night, and then they would. The nightmares kept coming. My wife did everything she could to help him, and she felt like she was making some headway," John says.

"If she was making progress, what changed?" I ask. "More importantly, how did he end up in DHS custody? I understand the government getting involved, but Homeland Security? That seems like a stretch. Why did they see him as a threat?"

"This happened two days before Cody was taken. A Kansas senator came to town with his son and daughter to promote a school initiative. His kids were meeting others at the event, and we were all there, including Cody. When the senator's daughter approached him, she was hit with a sudden headache. Her brother, who wasn't even nearby, experienced the same thing and described a disturbing vision. The sister then described a similar one. What they saw matched what our sons and other kids had been going through. The government was already aware of Cody's condition, though they believed it was just a cover for something else. We rushed our family out, but it quickly got out of hand. People were furious that we brought Cody. After that, the senator's office reached out to Homeland Security and claimed Cody was to blame. We're not sure what led them to that conclusion, but they insisted he be taken into custody, even though no one could clearly explain why. Two days later, DHS came and took him. We didn't know if he was staying nearby or sent far away. It devastated us. My wife fell into depression, and the stress ended our marriage. We now share custody of our kids. Part of me wishes we had never taken

Cody in, but I never blamed him. I don't know how he does what he does, but I've always believed it's a curse, not a gift," John says.

Melanie and I are both in tears; hearing someone finally speak with that kind of love for him… it hits hard. No amount of experience dulls that kind of pain.

"I really hate to hear what happened to you and your family. We only have a couple more questions to ask you. The next question I want to ask is about his sister, Ashley. Do you know what happened to her?" I ask.

"She was temporarily removed from her aunt and uncle until an investigation could be completed. They determined that Cody was the problem, so they kept him in foster care but reunited Ashley with her aunt and uncle. Phone calls weren't permitted when he first entered foster care. However, once he was placed with us, my wife started making progress with him, and they began allowing phone calls. I didn't know much about Ashley. All I knew was that she disappeared about a week after Cody was taken into DHS custody. She was never found. There was only one person of interest, and they interviewed him. I wasn't told how he was connected to Ashley. He claimed she had asked to go to Nevada, but he said no. There wasn't enough evidence to link him to her disappearance, so they let him go. I have no idea if what he said was true or if that's where she ended up. All I know is she went missing, and it devastated her aunt and uncle. Also, if you're thinking about trying to find them, they left town and didn't tell anyone where they were going," John said.

"So, there's a lot of mystery surrounding Ashley," says Melanie.

I'm glad we're getting a bit more insight. It helps fill in a few blanks, but honestly, it feels like for every revelation we get, two more questions come up. There are a couple of questions I still want to ask. I decide that I'll ask one more. I believe this question may hold a number of answers about some crucial details.

"I have one more question for you, John. What do you know about Cody and Ashley's parents?" I ask.

"To be honest, not very much. All I know is that their parents were arrested. We try to research what it is they were arrested for, but we've had no luck. My wife believes that the nightmares Cody is having begun sometime before their parents are arrested. She even assumes there's a direct connection between Cody and his parents. She believes that his parents may be indirectly causing these nightmares. However, children's services really didn't listen to us and didn't take her claim seriously."

"I see. That's horrible that they wouldn't listen to her. We have to find out what we can about their parents," I say to Melanie.

"John, I know Dr. Koraline says we only have one more question, but if you don't mind, I just want to ask one more, well, it's a few questions rolled into a central theme," says Melanie.

"Go ahead. But after this, that's all I'm doing," says John.

"You said that Cody gave them these nightmares. What exactly did they dream? Were they dreams composed of Cody's personal nightmares? Or were they their own nightmares but somehow Cody knew they would dream them?" Melanie asks.

"That's the weirdest thing surrounding him. Most of the time it would be his own personal nightmares, but people somehow end up dreaming their own interpretations of the nightmare. It's really hard to explain. This whole thing is hard to explain. However, they all have one thing in common: they all see Cody in their dreams. He doesn't speak, he doesn't do anything, he just stands there. No one knows how to take this, even us. The thing that's even more weird is the fact that even though we live with Cody for months, he never gives us nightmares."

They never have nightmares from him. Weird. Though, I start to develop a theory at this point. But I want to talk it over with Melanie before I fully go down this rabbit hole.

"Okay. John, we really are appreciative of the information that you have given us. There's so much going on that we don't have answers for. This will no doubt help us out greatly," I say to John.

"No problem. Now quickly, leave," John says.

We quickly get up and leave the house. We start making our way back to the hotel room.

"Has he really gotten that paranoid? He couldn't wait for us to leave," says Melanie.

"Well, how often do you have the US government come to your house and take custody of someone you love and never hear from them again?" I say.

"Yeah, I can't even imagine," Melanie says.

We make our way back to the hotel room. When we enter, I hear a loud pinging noise coming from my laptop. It's louder than usual. I go over to check it and see a message from Director Lynne. I open the chat program, and my mouth drops open.

"Dr. Koraline, what's wrong?" asks Melanie.

I turn the laptop around and show her the message:

Dir_Lynne: We've received a message from Gary. He isn't able to contact you. We're not even sure how he managed to reach us. He wants me to

pass along to you that no matter what, DO NOT GO TO KANSAS.
ESPECIALLY SHAWNEE. They're making their way there now, but
he doesn't know exactly where they are. Gary says he's not sure why they're
headed to Shawnee, but it has something to do with finding a big, locked box
that requires a weird, antique key to open it. Please take care of yourself.

"You're kidding! This is the worst-case scenario! Why is she coming after that chest?" Melanie asks.

"Maybe that chest is not only a way for us to get to the root of Cody's issues, but what if there's also a way to stop Salus?" I respond.

"That may be true, but we don't even know where to start looking for it," says Melanie.

"I don't know for sure, but I have a theory. What if John Robert isn't paranoid because of DHS? What if he's paranoid about someone finding out about the chest? What if the chest is in his home?" I suggest.

"That's a nice guess, but would John Robert even know or understand the meaning behind the chest? Also, I have a huge problem believing that Cody carried a huge chest from foster home to foster home," Melanie says.

"That may be true...but what if he didn't move it around? What if he only had it at that house?" I say.

"Why would you suggest that it's only been at that house?" Melanie asks.

"John said his wife made progress with Cody. Right? What if she bought that chest for him as a way to place 'memories' in the chest? Like, maybe some artwork or photos of a painful memory? What if he placed it in there as a way to help him cope and move on?" I suggest.

"You're making a lot of assumptions. Let's check and see if the chest is actually there before jumping to any more conclusions," says Melanie.

"You're right. But my gut is telling me that it's there. Also, I've done this a few times with previous clients."

Melanie and I get back into the car and I text John on Melanie's phone to let him know we need to come back over. He doesn't respond, but we head there anyway. We're on a mission. We're just ready to be done.

Chapter 19

Returned and Rejected

Even though Melanie texts John, he doesn't respond. John doesn't have read receipts turned on, so we have no idea if he even read the message. As we get closer to his house, we see a car speeding away from the street that leads to his place. At first, we don't think anything of it, but then it hits me.

"Wasn't that the car that was in his driveway?" I ask.

"Now that I think about it, yes, it was!" Melanie responds.

When we pull up to the house, there are fresh tire marks right in front. Now we're in a dilemma. How do we get into his house?

"Any ideas on how to get in?" Melanie asks.

"I think our best option is to break in," I suggest.

"Are you insane? You know we'd get in serious trouble if we did that!" Melanie exclaims.

"I know we would. But if law enforcement gets called, don't forget that we technically work under the Department of Homeland Security. We were told to use that as leverage if necessary. I don't want to break in either. I wish we had another choice. But we have to remember that Ashley is on her way to this town. We don't know if she knows exactly where the chest is or if she's playing the same guessing game we are. Either way, the faster we can confirm whether it's here, the faster we can get out," I say.

Melanie sighs and thinks for a moment. After a pause, she makes her decision.

"I'm not going in with you. But I'll keep an eye out here in case he comes back. I'll at least do that for you," she says.

"Okay. Thank you, Melanie."

I quickly get out of the car and begin searching for an unlocked door. I'm hoping that John, in his rush to leave, forgot to lock something. I check the front, back, and side doors… nothing. I even search for a spare key around the house, but again, no luck.

I start preparing myself, because I've never done anything like this before. I look around for something I can use to break a window. But then, I get lucky. I notice a window at the back of the house that's slightly open. There's no screen. I'm able to push it up and slip inside.

I land in the kitchen. It isn't messy, but it definitely looks neglected. I need to figure out the layout of the house. From the outside, I don't think there's a basement, but I check all the interior doors just in case. None of them lead down.

What I do know is that this house has an attic. The way the roof is shaped, there's at least some crawlspace up top. I search through the bedrooms and hallways. There's a master bedroom and three other rooms. Two of the bedrooms are down their own hall, and in that hallway, I find the retractable attic stairs. The string is short, so I grab a chair from the kitchen to reach it.

I reach up and try to pull the stairs down. They barely budge. It's like no one's used them in years. After a few more attempts, I finally get the stairs to come down and start making my way up. As my head rises into the attic, I look around and I can't believe what I see. About two feet from the entrance sits the same chest I've seen in my dreams.

I crawl all the way into the attic and pull the key from my pocket. I hold it in my hand for a moment, trying to wrap my mind around the possibility that maybe, just maybe, we're close to the end of all this. I step toward the chest and insert the key into the final keyhole, the one marked with a pocket watch symbol. It's difficult to turn. The watch portion of the key keeps resisting, but after a little effort, I manage to unlock it.

I hear the familiar sound of the interior locks moving, and I'm so excited. I'm finally starting to see the light at the end of this tunnel. I'm so ready to be done. Not just done for myself, but for Cody. Cody deserves to not be tortured anymore. I look forward to seeing what this last bit of information or memory is going to contain. The interior locks stop making noise. The key then dissolves into dust. I hear a clicking noise, as if the entire chest has just become unlocked.

I open the chest, bracing myself. I expect a blinding white light to burst out and fill the attic, something magical and dramatic. Maybe the room will start to shift, the air will hum, and I'll find myself in a place I do not recognize.

But nothing happens.

Not even a flicker. Only silence, dust, and the hollow interior of an old chest. I'm not sure if I have found the wrong one, or if, because I'm no longer inside a dream, I need to fall asleep again to understand what is really going on. Regardless, I'm confused, and I'm angry. Until I look inside the chest. What I find inside the chest is puzzling, and I don't know what to think.

There is another key. This key is also an antique key. I pick up the key. It doesn't look out of the ordinary like the four other keys. Just a traditional, antique key. I'm at a total loss on what this is supposed to mean. I put the key in my pocket and come back down to the main floor. I put everything back in order and go outside to Melanie.

"How did it go? What did you find out?" she asks.

"Nothing. I found out absolutely nothing. I opened the chest. I had no vision, no voices, nothing. The key dissolved, so if it was meant to open something else, we're out of luck. The only thing that was in there was another stupid key!" I exclaim.

"Seriously? That was it? I thought we were so close to being done with this whole thing and you are telling me we have another thing we have to uncover? Good grief," says Melanie.

We both feel so defeated. We have no idea what else to do, but then I pull the key back out. I stare at it, and that is when it hits me like a ton of bricks.

"Melanie, I don't know where we're supposed to go next. However, I just realized something. When Director Lynne contacted us, she informed us that Gary said she was looking for a big locked box that needs an antique key to open it," I say to Melanie.

"Yes. That is correct. Why are you bringing this up?" asks Melanie.

"What if the chest is not what she was looking for? What if the box is whatever this key goes to?" I ask.

"If that is true, then that would explain why nothing happened when you fully opened the chest?" asks Melanie.

"I don't know. The problem is, we don't have any leads on where we would find this box," I respond.

We start driving around town just trying to figure out some ideas of what our next step should be. While we are doing that, we get in contact with Matthew and Carly and fill them in on everything that is happening via text. Not long after we send off the text, we receive a phone call from Matthew.

"Yes, Matthew?" I reply.

"Listen to me. Carly, Dr. Hamilton, and I will be flying out to Kansas City to meet you and Melanie," says Matthew.

"Hold on. Is there not a ground stop in place?" asks Melanie.

"Yes, and it is still in place. However, we had something huge happen. Cody is no longer in Richmond. Also, the veil that was surrounding DC is gone," Matthew says.

"Well, at least we got some good news. But where is Cody going? Where are you taking him now?" I ask.

"Oh no, we didn't transport him. He left on his own, and we've been doing our best to keep him under surveillance, but Salus keeps interfering, making it difficult. We have no idea where he's headed. What's even more concerning is that while the veil over DC may have vanished, it's beginning to reappear elsewhere," said Matthew.

"Well, where at?" asks Melanie.

"It's coming right to where the two of you are located, in Shawnee," replies Matthew.

My heart drops. We don't know what to expect. We just know we need to find whatever this key unlocks and get out of

Shawnee as fast as possible. We look up and see a shadow creeping across the sky, swallowing the light bit by bit. The air feels heavier, colder. Whatever is coming, it's close. We know we're almost out of time.

"Okay. We have clues on another lead that we're trying to locate. Hopefully, we'll find it and be out of Shawnee by the time the three of you get here," I say.

"Hurry it up. Find what you need and get out of there ASAP," says Matthew.

"We'll do what we can," says Melanie.

After hanging up the phone, Melanie and I discuss what our next step is.

"I think our only option is to go back to John Robert's house and see if we can find any clues. I know it'll be a similar goose chase like at Gary's apartment, but maybe his wife left some documents there and we can go through them," I say to Melanie.

"I can't think of anywhere else to look or go, so let's head to his house," Melanie responds.

We make our way back to John Robert's house. This time, Melanie comes with me. I think the news of what happened in Washington is about to happen here has made her quickly get over her moral qualms. We enter through the same window I used earlier. We start looking around the house, trying to find clues. We split up. I look in the master bedroom and the bedroom next to it. Melanie takes the other hallway and looks at the other two bedrooms.

"Dr. Koraline, I think I found something. This bedroom looks like a partial office," says Melanie.

I come over to where she is and look in the room. There is a full-size bed by the wall to the left, and there's a medium-sized desk on the wall to the right. The desk has a couple of drawers; considering their size, they look like drawers that can be used as filing cabinets. We look through the drawers, but they're mostly empty. The only things in the drawers are envelopes marked with the word "Rejected," each one containing picture that had been sent back. We assume Cody is trying to send pictures to his aunt and uncle, but they're getting returned.

I look at the top of the desk and see a sticky note posted to a desk calendar. What's written on the sticky note catches my attention:

Surprisingly, the package Cody mailed was the only thing that has not been returned.

"Melanie, the sticky note says that a package Cody sent hasn't been returned. It doesn't say who it's sent to, but based on the returned letters we find here, I can only assume it's meant for his aunt and uncle," I say, studying the handwriting.

Melanie leans in for a closer look. "I think you're right. Do you think this package could be the box we're trying to find?"

I glance back at the note, wondering who wrote it and why they would leave it here in the first place.

"I think it's very possible. It looks like Cody is trying to send pictures to his aunt and uncle," I say to Melanie. "It's like he's trying to give them reminders that he still exists. Physical memories. I imagine this box may contain some type of physical memory. We might even be able to get an idea of what we're missing."

"Makes sense. I'll grab one of these envelopes so we can have the address. Hopefully someone is home and we can get what we need," says Melanie.

"If anyone has bought the house yet. Don't forget what John Robert said, the aunt and uncle move away. Regardless, we need to get into that house," I say to Melanie.

We promptly leave the house, and when we get outside, it's noticeably darker. We also start to notice some hues of purple striking across the sky. We are running out of time.

We quickly get to the car. Melanie puts the address into the phone. We see that it's a ten-minute drive from our current location. We quickly get on our way. I turn the radio on to see if I can get any updates before we lose contact with the outside world.

Government officials are still assessing the situation in Washington. Access to the city is now open to select personnel. The president, vice president, and Congress are confirmed safe. The most severe damage is at Homeland Security's headquarters, where Secretary Jones was killed and several others injured. It's unclear if this was an attack or a bizarre natural event. Meanwhile, strange purple lightning storms have hit cities across the U.S. and abroad, including Douglasville, Georgia; Cambridge, Massachusetts; Pottsville, Pennsylvania; Robinson, Texas; and Oxford in the UK. Damage has been reported, but most areas remain intact. We're working to verify new information and urge caution with social media claims. More coverage after the break.

I frantically call my mom. I want to hear if she's okay. Fortunately, she picks up and tells me she's fine. She says that although her current house was not damaged, my childhood home, just a couple of blocks away, was severely hit. No one was there at the time, but if someone had been, they wouldn't have survived. I tell Melanie what happened.

"I just don't understand. We are certain all of this is connected to Salus, but the places being attacked don't make any sense. I thought this was going to be like most alien or disaster movies where they hit the major cities. But this does not add up," I say.

"I wonder…" Melanie says.

"What?" I ask.

"Hold on." Melanie pulls over and checks the phone. I'm not sure what she is looking up, but her fingers are moving a mile a minute. I'm a little concerned that she thinks we have time for research when we are about to be stuck here. Still, I decide to trust her and wait.

"Okay, Dr. Koraline, I think I may know what's going on," Melanie says.

"Okay? I'm curious to hear your hypothesis," I respond.

"I don't think these attacks are random. I did some research on Secretary Jones. Do you know where he was raised?" Melanie asks.

"I have no clue," I respond.

"Potts, Pennsylvania," Melanie says.

"Really? That is odd," I say.

"While he works in DC, he has a home in Cambridge, Massachusetts. He helps teach a couple of short-term classes at Harvard," she says.

"Wait a minute, are you saying these attacks are targeting specific individuals, like Secretary Jones and me?" I ask.

"I believe so. I thought it was random too until you told me about your childhood home. This would also explain why Oxford got hit, since that is where you live and work. The only town I don't know the connection to is Robinson, Texas. Unless there is a link to you or Secretary Jones," Melanie says.

"I don't have a connection to that town. I'm not sure about Secretary Jones though," I respond.

"If these attacks are this specific, then we need to rush to that house and find that box. If Salus is willing to destroy towns just because of a personal connection, there is no telling what he will do when he gets here," Melanie says.

She jumps behind the wheel and speeds toward the house. When we arrive, it looks like it has been abandoned for a while. We walk up to the front door. It's locked, but the hinges don't look strong. After a bit of effort, we manage to break it down.

Inside, it feels surreal. The house looks like a rundown version of the one from our dream. The living room and hallway to the bedrooms are on the left, just as we remembered. We're not sure which room might hold the box, but both of us have a gut feeling it is the first room on the left, the one that looked like a child's room in the dream.

We step inside. The room is filled with scattered furniture, dusty boxes, old newspapers, and a few forgotten toys in the corners. Everything is worn but not destroyed, like someone left in a hurry. It's not the worst mess, but given how little time we may have, it is not ideal.

We quickly start moving items and searching the floor and walls for anything out of place. Ten minutes pass. Outside, it is

215

practically pitch black. We don't know how much time we have, if any. But we know we have to find that box.

We search every room. They're all empty. We are about to give up, but something keeps pulling us back to that first bedroom. We must have missed something. We return and inspect the space more thoroughly. Not even two minutes later, I spot something.

"There. That part of the wall, it looks patched up," I say.

"I saw a sledgehammer in the kitchen," Melanie says.

She grabs the small sledgehammer from the kitchen and starts tearing into the wall. I rip at the sheetrock around the holes she creates. After about five minutes, we find what we are looking for, a small box.

"Yes. Finally. We finally have it," I say.

"Quickly, let us open it. Let us see how we can put an end to this once and for all," Melanie says.

I reach into my pocket and pull out the key. I move to open the box...

"Open that box, and you are dead."

Chapter 20

Surrounded

Melanie and I slowly turn around. We see that it is Ashley. She is holding a detonator in her hand.

"If you open that box, I'm blowing up this house. The three of us will die here, as well as the horrible memories in this place," says Ashley.

We have no idea if she's bluffing or not, but I slowly put the box down. I still hold the key in my hand, though she signals for me to also put the key on the ground. So, I do. I have no intention of dying today.

I expect her to come and grab the box and key and then leave. However, she keeps standing there. I'm not sure what her intentions are since she's standing still. It looks like she's trying to fight her emotions. Her eyes are glassy, and her lips are pressed tightly together, like she is holding something back. I wonder if this is the first time she has been in this house since she left.

"Ashley…" Melanie says cautiously. "Where's Gary?"

Ashley does not answer right away. Her fingers tighten around the detonator as her eyes drop to the floor.

"He made his choices," she says quietly. "I made mine."

For a moment, something like regret flickers in her eyes, but it vanishes just as quickly.

"Let's just say he won't be interfering anymore."

Our expressions fall at the thought that Gary might no longer be alive. But the detonator in Ashley's hand quickly pulls our focus away from it.

"What do you want?" asks Melanie. "The box and key are on the ground."

Ashley walks over to the box and key. She stares at them for a long time.

"For years, I've wanted to know what was in this box. My aunt and uncle refused to show me. They even claimed that they got rid of it. However, Salus revealed to me not only that it still exists but that they had hidden it from me," says Ashley.

You can see the battle going on in her mind as she tries to determine whether she wants to open the box or not. I decide on an approach that may end up working against me. But it might be the only way that she can get closure. Maybe we can stop all this madness from happening.

"Ashley, would it be okay if I made a suggestion?" I ask.

Ashley stands there. She is still staring at the box. She doesn't look at me, but she slightly nods her head yes.

"What if we open the box together? I know your reasons are different from ours, but I also know you are searching for closure, and you deserve that. Still, while you are focused on justice, Salus is tearing the world apart. Taking revenge on a few people might feel satisfying, but what if that does not end the pain? Would you

218

really be willing to let everything fall into darkness for that?" I say to Ashley.

"If it means justice for my little brother, then yes, I'm more than okay with it," responds Ashley.

We stand there a little longer. She doesn't give a clear answer to my question about opening the box. I don't want to pressure her, so I choose to wait. I am glad I do, because after a moment, she begins to speak again.

"If we open the box together, then we both end up getting what we want. That doesn't feel fair to me. I don't understand why you even suggest it. I know you're desperate, but I honestly don't expect something so irrational from you," Ashley says, her voice edged with irritation.

I anticipated that she would respond in that manner. I really was hoping she wouldn't, but I also know the chances were very slim. So, I decide to add something to my offer. I already had this in mind, but I didn't want to offer it immediately. I want to see how she responds to my suggestion.

"How about this? Why don't we all see what's contained in this box, then I can give you something that you'd have a hard time refusing?" I say.

Melanie looks at me with a confused look. She is wondering what I am about to say next.

"I'm listening, but I highly doubt you have anything to offer that would convince me to go through with this deal," says Ashley.

I take a deep breath. I can't believe I'm about to say the following words. "Here's what I offer: after the three of us see what's in the box, I ask that you let my assistant Melanie go and you can also leave the house. I'll stay in the house, and I'll let you detonate it. You said you have bad memories here. I'm also the one who put your brother in state custody. So, if you blow up the house with me in it, your bad memories and one of the main people responsible all die, and maybe you can start to have some closure."

"Don't listen to her offer. This is pure madness! Killing her is not going to give you closure! Dr. Koraline dying is going to do absolutely nothing! I'm sorry, Dr. Koraline, but I can't allow this!" says Melanie.

"Melanie, I appreciate you trying to protect me. However, this is the only way," I say. I look over to Ashley and much to my surprise, she actually looks at me instead of continuing to stare at the box.

"I'll be honest with you, that's a very tempting offer. You know what, let me think about it for a little bit," says Ashley. Ashley starts to pace back and forth as she contemplates her options. Melanie rushes over to me. She definitely has a lot to say.

"ARE YOU MAD? This is the stupidest thing you could ever do! You know good and well this is not going to give this girl closure. All it'll do is embolden her!" says Melanie.

I grab the phone, open the notes app, and write a note for Melanie to discreetly see.

I know it won't give her closure. But it will give her a huge confidence boost. Overconfidence to be exact. With this overconfidence, she'll make more mistakes than ever. All of you should capitalize on her mistakes.

Melanie understands now why I'm doing this. She still isn't happy about it. She keeps insisting that we find another way. I wish we could find another way, but if giving up my life will give the rest of us a fighting chance to take down Salus, I'll do it.

Ashley stops her pacing and comes to both of us. "I accept your offer. I appreciate that you're willing to die for your mistakes. Justice would be served, but you still would not be forgiven," says Ashley.

She picks up the box and the key, looks at them for a moment, then inserts the key and turns it.

The Final Dream

As soon as the lock clicks open, the house explodes.

I definitely was not expecting that. But somehow, none of us are dead. The three of us are suspended in midair, floating as everything around us moves in slow motion. Splinters of wood and pieces of debris from the house hang around us, weightless and unreal. We somehow land on our feet. At that point, we're no longer in slow motion. However, the debris is still midair, circling us slowly like a slow-moving tornado. Though the debris spins around us, we can see beyond it. Melanie and I have no idea where we are, but Ashley's face says otherwise. Her eyes widen just slightly, and her mouth tightens like she is trying to keep something to herself. It is clear she recognizes the place.

"I didn't think I'd see this place again," says Ashley.

"What is this place?" asks Melanie.

"This place belongs to the person I ran away to see," answers Ashley.

"Was he a boyfriend or something?" I ask.

"Not my boyfriend, just a really good forger I found on the dark web," says Ashley.

I think we're close to putting the last pieces of this puzzle together.

"I tried to get answers about the whereabouts of my brother after DHS took him. I hit a wall with every attempt. Finally, I came up with a plan. I had no idea if it would work, but it did. After I found this forger on the dark web, I hitchhiked to Las Vegas so I could work odd jobs to get some cash. The amount he wanted was outrageous, but I didn't have a choice. I lived on the streets and worked any job I could find until I had about seven hundred dollars. That amount was nowhere close to what I needed, but the forger took pity on me after I told him why I needed the forged documents. I was able to get a fake Social Security card, a fake birth certificate, a fake high school diploma, and a fake bachelor's degree in psychology. My goal was to get hired by DHS and find out where my brother was," says Ashley.

Melanie speaks, and it sounds like she has the same question as me. "Why were you hired? Even with the education, they would need a reason to bring you on."

"The process wasn't easy. I got rejected every time. The only reason I was able to work as an assistant was because of what happened at my last interview," says Ashley.

"What happened?" I ask.

"I accidentally printed and signed my real name on a document. I didn't even catch it until I got the call two days later. The call was from Secretary Jones. He recognized my name from the files they had on Cody. He wasn't sure if I was the same Ashley, so he had me come in. I was in his office with two other people. I was intimidated, so I told them everything I had done. The other two people in the office wanted me arrested. Secretary Jones, however, overruled them. He proceeded to tell me where Cody was and that they weren't having any luck with research. He thought that maybe a familiar face would help Cody feel more relaxed, which in turn would give more answers to the researchers. He said Cody was in good hands and explained that I'd be brought on as an assistant, mostly to handle basic office tasks, given that my qualifications weren't real. He instructed me not to reveal my identity to the researchers or Cody. I was to wear a wig and glasses," says Ashley.

Wow. I can't believe that man was willing to go to that extreme just to get results. What was he thinking? Still, I try to reserve some judgment. I can't imagine the desperation of trying to figure out what is going on with Cody when there isn't any explanation within the realm of logic. When I think about it from that point of view, I start to understand his decision a little better. Also, I can't imagine the pressure he would've been under now that this whole thing includes a prominent senator's children.

Yeah, I shouldn't be too hard on him. I still don't agree with many of his decisions, but at the same time, I don't know what I would have done if this fell in my lap and I had to start from scratch. What's even worse is the fact that they can't get any answers. I still don't think he should have intensified the methods. If I had been part of this project from the beginning, I'd had advised them that this isn't something that can be wrapped up in a few years. It was always going to be a long-term study, and even then, there was a strong chance we would still be left with inconclusive results.

I turn my focus back to Ashley's story.

"I joined the project at sixteen. One of my few responsibilities was driving Cody between his foster home and the facility. Staying in disguise the entire time was incredibly difficult. I constantly fought the urge to reveal who I really was. I didn't think the disguise would work, but strangely, he never seemed to recognize me. He called me Lauren like everyone else. It broke my heart, but I was just grateful to see him every day. Things were fine until about a year later, when I saw his mental state decline. I noticed new people at the facility and asked Secretary Jones what was going on. He told me they were trying new methods on Cody and that it would be rough at first, but he'd adjust," Ashley says, tears falling down her face.

While Ashley tells her story, we remain surrounded by the debris of the house. But outside the vortex, the world keeps changing. As she continues speaking, we are pulled from one scene to the next, moving deeper into her memories. We feel surrounded, fully immersed in her story. Ashley stands still, staring ahead. I wonder what is on her mind. Did the house really blew up, or is that part of this strange dream? If it did blow up, are we alive but unconscious? Are we dead? There are a lot of unanswered questions about how we ended up in this dream state.

My concentration breaks when I hear sniffling coming from Ashley. She starts to cry heavily.

"Ashley, I do not approve of all of your methods. You still need to face the consequences of some of the things you have done, but I admire the love and determination you have for your brother," says Melanie.

"Yes, I completely agree with Melanie. You didn't let anything stop you from getting to your brother," I say to Ashley.

"Stop lying. I know the two of you are only saying this so you can get me to open up this letter," says Ashley.

"Letter? What letter?" asks Melanie.

Ashley holds up a letter. We do not know if it suddenly appears or if she discreetly pulls it out of her pocket. Regardless, we are baffled.

"This letter. This was in the box. It flew out of the box when the house explodes, but I grabbed it and held onto it," says Ashley.

"Ashley, we really mean it. We really do admire your love and determination. However, there is always a right way and a wrong way to go about things," I say to Ashley.

I'm not sure if Ashley believes us or not. I do get the sense, however, that she does not like us telling her that wrong things done with good intentions still deserve consequences.

Ashley looks at me and then at Melanie and says, "You now know what I had to go through in order to see my brother."

She then looks right at me and asks, "Is there anything else you want to know before you die?"

I decide to ask her a question that has been bugging me for days.

"Yes, I have a really big question for you. Who is Salus? How do you find out about him and contact him?"

Ashley sits down on the ground. She doesn't sit in a way like she is going to refuse to answer. Instead, it is more of a "this may get complicated so listen well" posture

"You probably will not believe me, but I honestly have no idea where Salus comes from," says Ashley.

"Stop pretending you do not know! You had to have found out about him and reached out so he could help you get revenge on everyone!" I say to her, my voice rising with frustration.

"Listen, Dr. Koraline, I'm being honest with you. The first time I have contact with him is through a dream I have three months before I drove Cody to the VLA. He is terrifying. The only thing he tells me is that he's a being whose only goal is to find what he calls 'Dream Masters.' He says that a Dream Master is an individual who is able to manipulate dreams. He says some are able to do it at their own will, some cannot control when it happens, and some have it both ways. He says he faintly picks up Cody's strength. I tell him about the pain and suffering Cody is going through. He says if I'm able to get Cody near some type of transmitter device so he can fully detect his power, then he will end his suffering without harming him. He even says that he can give me some of his power to help deliver justice. You must understand, I'm desperate, so I did what he asked. He never tells me why he is tasked with finding Dream Masters, so I have no idea what his intentions are," says Ashley.

Ashley unfolds the letter. Melanie and I see a young Cody writing a letter on a desk through the debris. Ashley reads the letter aloud.

Dear Ashley,

I really miss you. It's been so hard having no contact with you. I just want to know why you haven't written me back. I've sent so many letters, but you haven't responded to a single one. I really need you. I'm having flashbacks again. This flashback is from before I started having these dreams. It was the time when Dad nearly choked me unconscious and then Mom tried to drop me in the tub soon afterwards. It was horrible.

Besides the flashback, nothing else has really changed. I'm still having the weird thing going on with my dreams and it's impacting the people around me. People at school are scared of me. My last few foster parents want me out of their houses. I'm miserable, I'm down all the time, I don't know what to do.

Please respond to me. I love you, and I hope you still love me.

The three of us are very emotional and in tears by the time she finishes reading the letter.

Wow. Just wow. Never in my life have I ever felt more guilt than I do in this moment. Well, I do think that Cody would've ended up in state custody eventually, but I still feel horrible that I'm the one who started the process. I can't help but think where Cody would be if I hadn't rushed to judgment all those years ago. I created such a mess. To think, this whole time I thought I did a great deed, and all I really do is make a brother question if his sister still loves him.

Ashley's sadness quickly turns to rage. She looks straight at me. I expect her to scream or hit me. I'm bracing for just about anything. But once again, my naïveté catches me off guard. The next words out of her mouth make me freeze.

"Time to die," Ashley says in a low voice. She lifts her hands as if she's about to deliver the final blow. But then, she suddenly drops her hands and falls to her knees. I feel a presence behind me, and before I can even turn to look, Ashley speaks in a very broken voice.

"Cody?"

Chapter 21

The Completed Puzzle

We look behind us and see that it is indeed Cody. Ashley's entire demeanor changes. She runs past us and goes straight to Cody. She hugs him very tightly for a long time.

"Cody, I can't believe you're here. I've done so much for you. I hope you will appreciate what I was about to do next," says Ashley.

"That is the reason I showed up. I can't let you do this. I can't let you hurt anyone else," says Cody.

Ashley lets go of Cody. She looks at him in disbelief.

"What do you mean? Dr. Koraline is the reason all of this is happening. She did not believe us. She is just as responsible as everyone else," exclaims Ashley.

"Yes, she played a big role in putting us on this path. There is no doubt about that. But we cannot go around getting revenge on everyone. Do you realize how much worse my nightmares have become because of you? Yes, Salus is the one doing the harm, but my body is his host. His thoughts and actions are mixed with mine.

I've been carrying this guilt for months. I hated how I was treated in Socorro, and I know you did too. But you were assigned to pick me up. Why did you not just take me and disappear? That would have been so much easier, and no one would have gotten hurt," says Cody.

Ashley stands there in disbelief. She expected Cody to be thankful for everything she has done for him. Instead, he tells her that she only made things worse and added to his trauma, even if she did not mean to.

Cody continues, "We both hated how our parents treated us. Especially me. I have been struggling to cope. These dreams were my only escape from the flashbacks. But over time, the dreams stopped helping. For some reason, I'm making other people have dreams now. So, I'm not just dealing with my own pain, I must be afraid of what I'm doing to others. Then you bring in this being to help me? What were you thinking?"

"He said he would get revenge. He even promised he would get rid of your nightmares. Secretary Jones is gone. The people in Socorro are gone. Our parents were released from prison and moved to Robinson, Texas. They are dead now. You should be thanking me," says Ashley.

Well, that at least explains why Robinson, Texas was targeted.

"Ashley, why would you trust someone, whether human or something else, who contacts you and takes an interest in me without even understanding the full situation?" asks Cody.

"Because we have been wronged so badly. Our parents abused you terribly and I couldn't stop it. Dr. Koraline didn't believe us and I couldn't change her mind. The state took you away and I couldn't stop the caseworkers. I was tired of feeling helpless. So, I took action," says Ashley.

She looks like she wants to say more, but she stops herself and starts crying again. She looks down at the floor where her tears fall. After a pause, she speaks again.

"When I did all this, I never thought you would get hurt. I never thought Salus would take control of you. I thought he would do what I asked and leave you alone. Hurting you was never the plan. But Cody, I still truly believe that if I kill Dr. Koraline, everything will end."

Cody goes over to Ashley and gently raises her head so she's looking straight at him. "If this is the route you feel you must take, then I do not truly know you. No one else is going to die today if I can help it."

Cody violently pushes Ashley away and yells to Melanie and me, "Hold on. You're getting out of this dream." He lifts his hands toward both of us, and the next thing we know, we are flying up and through the air. It's a terrifying experience. Both of us are screaming as we travel dangerously fast through the air. The area around us suddenly becomes a bright white. When the whiteness fades, Melanie and I are standing in the room we were in before we entered the dream.

"Let's get out of here, fast," says Melanie.

We both rush out of the house. As soon as we get outside, we receive a phone call. It is Carly. I answer and put it on speaker.

"Hey, where are the two of you located?" asks Carly.

"We are at Cody's childhood home. However, we are about to leave and get out of town," says Melanie.

"You cannot. The entire town is sealed with the same veil that surrounded DC," says Carly.

We're in such a rush to get out of the house that we don't even notice that Shawnee is completely surrounded by the black and purple veil.

"If we are not able to leave town and we are separated from the outside world, how are you calling us?" I ask.

"We arrived in Kansas City and came to Shawnee. We've been trying to contact you for a couple of hours now," says Carly.

What? A couple of hours? How long were we in this dream? I look at my phone and see that seven hours have passed. How? I don't have time to dwell on that. I need to find out what the next step in our plan is.

"So, if we cannot leave, where do you want us to go?" I ask.

"Meet us at—"

Before Carly can fully answer, Salus emerges from the house with Ashley close behind. At first, he appears to be a normal height, but then the black and purple veil begins firing bolts of lightning at him. Each strike causes him to grow larger. Massive. The only thing I can compare his size to is Godzilla, or at least how I imagine Godzilla would look in real life. He's a towering, monstrous figure made entirely of shifting blackness, like a void given shape. You cannot see details, only the sharp outline of claws and limbs and those glowing red eyes burning through the darkness. Carly and the others show up a minute after Salus emerges.

"Oh man, what is going on?" asks Dr. Hamilton.

Salus stands completely still in the distance, not moving an inch. We quickly fill the three of them in on what is happening. We leave out a few details but give them the overall picture. Ashley, however, begins walking toward us.

"Where is Cody?" I ask.

"Well, since he was not appreciative of what I have done for him, I let Salus fully absorb him. Maybe one day he will learn to be appreciative of what I've done for him," answers Ashley.

She's a monster! How could she let that thing consume her brother? Maybe she's so consumed by her rage and desire for revenge that she doesn't even think about what she's doing. Regardless, it's clear to me what I need to do. However, that's going to have to wait, because Ashley starts giving Salus orders.

"Kill them. Destroy everything in this town."

Salus lets out a loud roar. That is the most terrifying noise I've ever heard in my life. We all decide that we need to at least regroup in another part of town. We quickly get into our vehicles and take off. Salus is shooting purple lightning and the veil toward us. Fortunately, he's missing us for the most part. However, we are realizing how many other people's lives we are putting at risk. Homes and businesses along our route are getting completely destroyed.

"We need to find an area that has the least amount of people," says Melanie.

"I agree. Text Matthew and tell him that we need to go..." Before I can finish what I'm saying, Salus hits both of our vehicles.

Our car flips once, then again. Metal groans, glass shatters, and for a few heart-stopping seconds, everything spins out of control. When we finally slam to a stop, upside down and gasping for air, I can hear the ticking of the engine and the ringing in my ears.

I squint, trying to get my bearings. My hands tremble, but I can move them. As far as I can tell, nothing is broken. Melanie groans beside me but gives me a nod. She is alive, dazed, but alert. Somehow, we are okay. I twist around and look through the cracked windshield. The other vehicle has taken a much harder hit. It has flipped several times and landed on its side in the distance, with smoke curling from beneath the hood.

Panic surges through me. We scramble out of the car and run toward them as fast as our bodies will allow. Dr. Hamilton is lying on the ground near the wreck. Blood trickles from his forehead, but he is conscious and murmuring our names.

But Carly and Matthew…

They're still in the car.

No movement.

I freeze, staring, heart pounding in my ears. I already know.

Flames light up the horizon as Salus tears through the town, ripping up streets and sending debris flying through the air. Power lines snap and spark, cars are overturned like toys, and buildings crumble beneath the force of his massive limbs. The once quiet neighborhood is becoming unrecognizable with each step he takes. We want to mourn the loss of Carly and Matthew. However, we also know that we need to figure out a way to stop this. After we pull Dr. Hamilton from the wreckage, we ask him if he is okay. He insists that he's fine.

"So, what do you think, Doctor? What are our options?" I ask.

"Salus. I notice that his form does not seem to be solid," says Dr. Hamilton.

"What do you mean his form is not solid?" asks Melanie.

"His whole body seems to be a huge black void. What if we go into the void and find Cody? Perhaps that will lessen Salus's power, and we can then take him out completely," says Dr. Hamilton.

"That's a good plan. Salus is powerful, but it does seem that he feeds off Cody to become stronger. How should we do this?" asks Melanie.

"I have a plan. The two of you need to find somewhere safe to lay low," I say to them. "I'm going to take our vehicle and drive it straight toward Salus. The engine is still running, and it might be just functional enough to get me close. I know there is a good chance he could strike me again, but if I can make my maneuvers unpredictable and fast, maybe I can get close enough before he reacts. The goal is to reach that void as quickly as possible. It is risky, but it may be the only shot we have."

"Do you think we're going to let you do this by yourself? You are crazy," Melanie says.

"Melanie is right. You shouldn't do this by yourself," says Dr. Hamilton.

"Listen, with Carly and Matthew gone, we need to have a Plan B in case this does not work. We can't get any help from the outside. We are all that is left. That way, if things don't work out, the two of you can come up with something," I say to them.

I start running to the car, but Melanie is running behind me.

"Dr. Geneva Koraline. You're not going by yourself!" she yells to me.

She grabs my shoulder and turns me around. I look at her and say, "Thank you for being such a great help to me. I also want to say that I'm sorry."

"Sorry for what?" says Melanie.

I ball up my fist, and with all of my might, I punch her. She falls to the ground. I take advantage of her being on the ground and quickly jump into the car and take off.

I feel really horrible for doing that to her, but I know that with so few of us working against Salus, we definitely need to have back up in case this doesn't work. I'm extremely nervous. I even think to myself, what am I doing? However, I know there is no turning back now. Trying to get to Salus is more difficult than I realize. There are no cars on the road so I don't have to dodge traffic, but since he has already done so much destruction, I have to watch out for debris scattered all over the roads. There is some debris I cannot avoid and I have to drive over it. The car does not get damaged every time, but I can tell the repeated impacts are wearing it down fast.

I finally get to Salus. I see Ashley, who is staring at me. I'm not sure what she's saying, but it looks like she's yelling and pointing at me. I think she's trying to get Salus to stop me.

I see an attack of his hit inches behind my vehicle. It really scares me, but fortunately, his attack sends me even closer to his body. I put the pedal to the floor. I'm getting so close. Then finally, I enter his body, the terrifying black void. As soon as I enter it, I slam on the brakes. I almost crash into a tree, but fortunately, I stop in time. I get out of the car and I see that I'm in some type of forest. It is a very strange forest, fairly dense with numerous trees.

"This is so weird," I say to myself.

I'm not sure where to go until I see something in one particular direction of the forest that catches my attention. There is a dim, bluish green light and I decide to start heading toward it.

As I walk, I watch where I step. The ground is covered with leaves, and I don't know what to expect being inside this terrifying being.

While making my way through the forest, I come across a path. At first glance, there is nothing remarkable about it, but something feels off. I notice the trees on both sides stop abruptly, and their roots don't cross onto the path. They all just cut off right before reaching it. I step onto the path and immediately spot the strange light straight ahead. I begin walking toward it. At first, I take my time, moving cautiously, but then it hits me. Every second counts. People in Shawnee are dying right now. I need to find Cody, and I need to do it fast.

The light continues to grow brighter the closer I get. I have no idea what to expect inside the strange light, but I work up every bit of courage I have to face it head on. Five minutes pass, and I finally get to the source of the light. There is a tree in front of this light. I stand there for a little bit. I know the sense of urgency that I should have. However, all of this is still so strange to me. My whole world has been turned upside down in a matter of a few days. It still feels so surreal. I take a deep breath and step past the tree line.

When I step past the tree line, I cannot believe my eyes. I'm in a strange environment, surrounded by water. However, I can still breathe, but it is a very heavy type of breathing. I can walk, but I have trouble. It is so strange, especially when I remember that this environment reminds me of the other embassy staffer's dream. Chris, if I remember his name correctly. Crazy, I didn't realize at the time that both Chris and Lea's dreams are foreshadowing what's to come. As I take in the environment around me, I notice Cody sitting on the ground with his head resting on his knees. It's him, not the younger version I have seen in previous dreams, but Cody as he is now. He's wearing a pink onesie, and there's something vulnerable in the way he sits. I quietly sit down beside him, and we start to talk.

"Cody, I never got a chance to thank you for saving our lives earlier. That was really sweet of you. That also took a lot of courage to stand up to your big sister," I say to Cody.

"Thanks. But Salus still won," says Cody.

"Not if we don't let him. We still have a chance," I reply.

"There's no way. I'm fully absorbed in this place now. There's no way we can stop him," says Cody.

"Fully absorbed in this place? What do you mean by that?" I ask.

"When Salus first started to occupy my body and mind, a small part of me was kept in this prison. Little by little, he kept putting more of me in here. I had a little bit of strength to fight when you and Melanie were in trouble, but I knew that after I used up that strength, he would take me over completely," says Cody.

"I see. Why can't we leave now?" I ask.

"I can't," he replies.

"Why can't you? Are you too physically weak to leave? Do you need my help?" I ask.

"It's not that. He designs this prison so a human being has to be in it at all times. If there is only one human being, the seal closes on the inside and you can't escape," he says.

"That puts us in a sticky situation, doesn't it?" I say.

"It does. So, Salus wins. Ashley wins. I never meant for any of this to happen. I just want to not have to relive those horrible memories again. I don't know why I keep giving people dreams. I don't mean to make my sister feel like she needs to go on a revenge tour," he says.

"None of this is your fault, Cody. Don't take responsibility for Ashley's actions. She makes her own choices and she must deal with the consequences," I say to Cody.

I try to think of how to execute my plan. I have one in place before I enter into the dark void of Salus. I just need to know the logistics of what I'm working with.

"Cody, here's what we are going to do. You say one human has to be in here at all times, right?" I ask.

"Yes. Why are you asking?" Cody asks.

"Here's the plan. You get out of here, and I'll stay behind. Once you are out of the void, use my phone to contact Dr. Hamilton to reach Mealnie. Tell her to bring the key with the pocket watch on the handle. I always thought that key was strange, actually all of them are, but I think I finally understand why that one has a pocket watch. I believe time is Salus's greatest weakness. That key might be the tool we need to destroy him. So, once you have it, come back with Melanie and Dr. Hamilton, and together we will end this. You'll be free, and we can all figure out what comes next," I say.

"Wow. Dr. Koraline, you really are smart. That sounds like it may work, but what if it doesn't work?" says Cody.

"I know this seems scary, Cody, but sometimes you have to take a leap of faith. Will you take that leap of faith, Cody?" I ask.

He has to think on it. I can tell that he's really going over everything in his mind. He stands up and I stand up alongside with him. He looks at me and says, "Will this really help bring this all to an end?"

"Yes, Cody, it should."

I give him the burner phone and we look to see if we can find the boundary of this prison. We find some distortions in the water patterns that surround this place.

"Okay, Dr. Koraline, I'll be back! Thank you!" says Cody.

"You're welcome, Cody!" I say.

Cody takes a minute to calm himself down, and then he goes through the boundary into the forest.

Melanie

Ow! I can't believe that woman hit me. What nerve. My jaw is sore, but I'll be okay. I help Dr. Hamilton up. "I don't care what she says. I think we should be nearby, just in case she needs backup."

"I agree. I'm not sure why she's so eager to do this alone. What she said does make some sense, but it's also foolish," says Dr. Hamilton.

We look around to see if we can find a vehicle, and there's a house not too far from us with three cars out front. I really don't want to pull a Dr. Koraline and break into the house for keys, but time is critical. Dr. Hamilton and I try the front door and are surprised to find it unlocked. It does not look like anyone is home, so we should be good. We start going through the house, searching for keys. It takes about five minutes, but we finally find a set that belongs to the SUV parked outside.

"Let us try not to wreck any more vehicles today, okay?" says Dr. Hamilton.

"Tell that to Salus," I respond.

Right before we head out, we feel a rumble. It's not constant, more like thudding footsteps. This cannot be happening. He's coming toward us.

"Let us get out of the house now. The debris from his attack will be deadly if we stay inside," says Dr. Hamilton.

We both run out the back door and look behind us. Salus is right there. Ashley is close by, running toward us, but she doesn't get too close.

"I have no idea what Dr. Koraline is up to, but I'm tired of the two of you meddling in things that do not concern you. Salus, kill them," says Ashley.

"With pleas… Aaaaaah!"

We look up at Salus, startled. His body jolts violently, like something had stricken him from the inside. His arms flail as if fighting against an invisible force. Shadows ripple across him, and his form begins to flicker, shifting between solid and unstable. Whatever is happening, it is powerful and it is stopping him from completing the command.

"Salus! Salus! What's going on? Salus, answer me!" Ashley yells.

She runs to the front of the house where Salus is. We follow her. We cannot believe what we see.

Cody is stepping out of the black void of Salus.

"Cody! What are you doing out here?" Ashley screams in rage.

She charges at him, but I reach her first and shove her down to the ground. Dr. Hamilton and I hurry to Cody, who's out of breath.

"Melanie, Dr. Hamilton, I'm so glad I found you. Dr. Koraline is still inside. She told me to tell you, Melanie, to bring the key with the pocket watch. That key is the secret to destroying Salus," says Cody.

I hear what Cody is saying, but I'm confused.

"Cody, are you sure she said the pocket watch key?" I ask.

"Yes, that's what she said. Salus trapped me in a strange prison and designed it so that at least one person, especially someone with my abilities, had to stay inside at all times. That is how he fed off my powers. She stayed behind so I could return with the key."

He must have misheard. He has to. The pocket watch key dissolved when Dr. Koraline used it, so there is no way that…

Oh no…

That is why she wanted to go alone.

Dr. Koraline

Yes… my plan is working.

Not the plan I told Cody, but my hidden plan. I have no idea if that key is actually a weapon. I only told him that so he'd leave. I already figured out that Salus is feeding off Cody's power. Now that Cody is no longer in his grasp, Salus should be weakened. The things he was capable of, like forming a massive black void for his body or entering dreams, should either be gone or at least severely limited. Once he is weakened, they can destroy him for good, which would mean I'd be killed in the process.

That thought terrifies me when I first came up with this plan, but I realize this is the least I can do for that kid after everything I have put him through. So, I remain in the prison and wait.

Chapter 22

Picking Up the Pieces

Melanie

Dr. Hamilton walks over to me after noticing the look on my face. He can tell I'm worried and senses that something is wrong.

"What's the issue? What's going on?" asks Dr. Hamilton.

"Dr. Koraline... I think she plans to sacrifice herself," I answer in a whisper.

He looks stunned by what I've just said. For a moment, he seems unsure how to respond. Then he takes a breath, steadies himself, and begins to process the situation with a more focused expression.

"She must be doing this because she doesn't have any powers. Which means he will become as fragile as a normal human being. I don't want to take her life along with Salus', but with the way he is transforming so quickly, we may not have a way to save her," says Dr. Hamilton quietly.

"Okay," I say, tears beginning to form. "What do we do?"

"Follow my lead," Dr. Hamilton says under his breath. Then his tone shifts; louder, sharper, almost accusing.

"Melanie! We were just in that house behind us. I think I saw something fall out of your pocket."

I catch on quickly to what he is doing and "check" my pockets.

"It's not in my pocket! It must have slipped out! Cody, we were mostly in the back rooms of the house. Can you go inside and check if you can find the key while we keep Ashley and Salus distracted?" I say to Cody.

"Of course!" he replies.

He hurries into the house to look for the "key." As he searches, Salus keeps shrinking and gradually takes on a more humanlike form. His eyes glow red, and he wears a trench coat, but his entire body remains black, with only the outline visible. Ashley stays fixated on him.

"What do we do next?" I ask.

"Go to the vehicle I was in and pull out Matthew's body. Grab the gun from his holster. When you get it, shoot at Salus quickly. I know this is a lot to ask, and if you can't do it, I will. I'm just worried my injuries will keep me from getting a clean shot. Either way, we have to do it before Cody comes back. Yes, we will have a lot to explain, but I'd rather explain after Salus is neutralized than before," he says.

I nod and head to the vehicle. Ashley is still distracted, panicking over Salus losing power. When I reach the vehicle, I pause. I have never handled a dead body before; I don't feel ready for this. But then a screech from Salus jars me back to reality. My adrenaline spikes.

I rush to the driver's side and unbuckle Matthew's seatbelt. Thankfully, I do not have to pull him out. His handgun is easy to reach.

Gun in hand, I quietly approach Salus. He screeches again, furious. I've fired guns on a range, but I never imagined I would be here, aiming at a being like this, and at someone who has become a friend. I know I have to get closer. This will be the hardest thing I've ever done.

I get into position, ready to fire, but I freeze. I'm not sure I can do it. Then I look at the destruction around me. I realize that right now, in this moment, I can stop the world from falling apart.

I decide to count to five: One... two... I switch the safety off... three... four... everything around me goes silent. I can barely hear my own breathing.

"Dr. Geneva Koraline, I'm so sorry."

Five.

I speed walk closer to Salus and fire seven shots into him. Salus stops moving. The shrieking ends. He then falls to the ground. Ashley starts screaming bloody murder. "WHAT HAVE YOU DONE?"

The screaming catches Cody's attention, and he runs outside the house. He sees Salus dying on the ground and the gun still in my hand. I flip the safety back on, but my fingers are trembling. The gun slips from my grasp and hits the ground with a dull thud.

I collapse, sobbing uncontrollably. My chest feels tight, and I can barely breathe. I rock back and forth on my knees, my hands shaking as I try to make sense of what I've just done. I have killed Salus... and with him, Dr. Koraline.

The weight of it crushes me. Cody runs toward Dr. Hamilton and me. "WHAT DID YOU DO? DR. KORALINE IS GONE! WHY DID YOU DO THIS?" he exclaims.

"Cody, there was no other choice. Dr. Koraline knew this," I say to Cody.

"YOU'RE LYING! YOU'RE LYING TO ME!" says Cody.

"Cody, the key that she told you to ask about, it doesn't exist anymore. She only said that to save your life," I say as I try to comfort him.

"STOP LYING TO ME!" he says.

This is so hard to deal with. I hate that we have to lie to him, but it has to be done.

Dr. Koraline

I patiently wait to see how this will all end. I still feel optimistic, but I would be lying if I said it doesn't terrify me knowing that I'll be dying soon. I regret giving Cody my phone. I don't know if I have service in here, but it would have been nice to say goodbye to my mom. I start crying again, but then I begin to think to myself. I have lived an amazing life. I have done so much and made a difference to so many people.

As I sit lost in thought, the ground beneath me begins to tremble. Suddenly, a stark white landscape appears, just like in my first dream. The only difference this time is the air. Every second, it feels like there is less of it in the room. Why is this happening? Unless they did it. They must have succeeded. I knew they could do it. While I feel excited that they won, I also begin to panic because I'm starting to suffocate.

It becomes scarier with every breath I take, especially knowing that any one of them could be my last. I calm myself down and lay on the ground. This is it. My life is coming to an end. The air continues to thin. I feel myself drifting in and out of consciousness. I'm scared. There is no denying that. But at the same time, I feel a deep sense of peace. Knowing that my life is coming to an end while doing something selfless, something that truly matters, brings me a strange kind of comfort.

I'm not just fading away without purpose. I'm choosing to protect others, to give them a fighting chance, even if it costs me everything. That thought, even in the face of death, fills me with a quiet sense of fulfillment. I may be afraid, but I know I'm going out doing the right thing.

Oh man. Breathing is so hard. I can't even think clearly anymore. I wish my mom were here with me right now. In this moment, I just want her. I want her to hold my hand and tell me it is going to be okay, even if it is a lie.

I think… I will just… close my eyes now.

Melanie

In a matter of minutes, Salus vanishes completely. Not a single trace of him remains. Dr. Hamilton and I scan the area around us, but he's nowhere to be found. However, what happens next quickly grabs our attention.

"Look, Melanie, the sky is starting to clear," says Dr. Hamilton.

I look around me. The veil that surrounded Shawnee is completely gone. Unfortunately, a good portion of the city is in complete ruins. Emergency vehicles are making their rounds to the various places of devastation. Cody is sitting on the ground, still processing what has just taken place. I try to tell him the truth, but I know he is going to need time. I decide to just let him have his space for now. Dr. Hamilton comes over to me. He has a determined look on his face.

"Dr. Hamilton, what do we do now?" I ask.

"I honestly don't know. There's so much that'll have to happen over the coming months. I know we both, along with the rest of the researchers, are going to be questioned, especially since the people in charge of this crazy project are all dead," responds Dr. Hamilton.

"That is true. I don't know if I can handle all of that. I was simply a photographer in this process. I can't answer any of the technical aspects of the project," I say.

"To be fair, Melanie, neither can I, nor can the researchers who were working the project. We were not making any headway," says Dr. Hamilton.

"Good point. What do we do now?" I ask.

"Go to the hotel room and gather your stuff and Dr. Koraline's. Meet me outside your hotel room and I'll pick you up. I'll call and we'll see what DHS wants us to do," says Dr. Hamilton.

"What about Ashley?" I ask.

We look to where Ashley had been, but we see that she's gone. We didn't even see her leave. Electricity is out in the area. I guess she slipped away under the cover of darkness. There's no telling where she's heading next.

Dr. Hamilton, Cody, and I get into our recently "acquired" SUV and he takes numerous detours to get to the hotel. What is supposed to be a ten-minute drive ends up taking around thirty minutes. Cody is silent the entire time. I wish I knew what's on his mind. Regardless, I'm just glad he got into the truck. Dr. Hamilton drops me off and I go inside. When I open the hotel room, I fall to the floor crying. Seeing Dr. Koraline's stuff is overwhelming. I don't know what to do with it. I guess I could send it to her mom. Oh no, I have to inform her mom that her daughter is dead.

It's hard to fully grasp the weight of what has been lost. Dr. Koraline is gone, her life ultimately claimed by a single decision she made years ago. Gary, our trusted informant, risking everything to deliver the truth we so desperately needed. Reflecting on their sacrifices makes it all the more difficult to accept that it has all been for the sake of bringing peace to one young boy.

It takes me a while to get everything packed. I had to take so many breaks as I deal with what has happened. I do get it done eventually. The last thing I pick up is the laptop she received from MI6. Before I leave the hotel room, I hear the ping go off. I know that it's a message from MI6. I sit down on the bed and open the laptop. To my surprise, it isn't locked. I see the message in the chat program.

Dir_Lynne: Is everything ok? We heard that there was a massive phenomenon taking place in Kansas.

Dir_Lynne: Please respond!

I decide to chat back.

Dr_Kor: Dr. Koraline sacrificed herself to save the boy, Cody. The phenomenon should be over, not just here, but around the world. The secrets of the Dream Master have finally been revealed.

Chat ended.

There's no response. I don't know if they are trying to verify what I told them or if they suspect Dr. Koraline has been compromised. I truly have no idea. But one thing I do know is that I have to destroy the laptop. I will not let myself be connected to whatever MI6 is involved in.

Though I begin to hesitate, my curiosity gets the better of me. I genuinely want to know what MI6 plans to do with the information it has gathered. But before I get the chance to explore the laptop, they remove the user account. I close it, still uncertain about what to do next. Whatever decision I make, it'll have to wait for another time.

I don't know what the future holds. I don't know if research on Cody will continue or if they'll simply let him be. I don't know if Ashley will go into hiding or try to come after us. So many things are going to happen over the coming months.

What I do know is that we finally figured out why Cody started having these crazy dreams. We may not fully understand how those dreams latch on to other people, but we got a glimpse into his mind and saw what kind of trauma he was facing. Dr. Koraline made a grave mistake years ago, but I believe she redeemed herself by saving Cody's life and taking his place.

I stand up from the bed and walk toward the door with our stuff. I see Dr. Hamilton sitting in the SUV, waiting on me. I turn around, look at the hotel room one last time, and close the door. I walk over to the truck, place everything in the back, and watch as he steps out to speak with me.

"What now?" I ask.

"DHS will be here shortly. They say they do not know for sure what the next steps are, but for now, Project Lion's Tears is no more," says Dr. Hamilton.

"That is a relief. What is going to happen to Cody?" I ask.

"I don't know, but they say that if it is true what I told them about what happened in Socorro, they don't want to order any more research or experimentation on him," says Dr. Hamilton.

"That is great news!" I say.

Dr. Hamilton starts up the SUV, the engine rumbling to life as we begin our drive toward a makeshift emergency operations center that has been set up to await the arrival of the Department of Homeland Security. The mood inside the vehicle is heavy but calm, a fragile stillness hanging in the air. Cody, still in the back seat, has drifted into a deep sleep. His breathing is steady, his body finally at rest after everything we have endured.

As I look at him, I cannot help but reflect on the long and turbulent path that brings us here. The Dream Master has been through more than most could ever imagine. Sixteen years of chaos, mystery, and silent suffering have shaped his story. But now, for the first time, there is a glimmer of hope that he might finally be able to lay his burdens down. After everything he has faced, the thought that peace might be within reach feels both surreal and deeply comforting.

The end.

About the Author

Charles Prince was born in West Germany and raised in Lithia Springs, Georgia. At sixteen, while still a junior in high school, he self-published his first book, beginning a lifelong passion for writing. He has since continued to develop stories that reflect his creative interests and imagination.

He now lives in the Cincinnati area with his wife and works as a houseparent while continuing to pursue his writing career.

cmprince.com

Instagram.com/indiewritercmp